Truth or Dare

Copyright © 2025 Patti Petrone Miller All rights reserved
TRUTH OR DARE

The characters and events portrayed in this book are fictitious. Any similarity to real persons, living or dead, is coincidental and not intended by the author.

No part of this book may be reproduced, or stored in a retrieval system, or transmitted in any form or by any means, electronic, mechanical, photocopying, recording, or otherwise, without express written permission of the publisher.

Cover design by: Grady Earls
Printed in the United States of America

The urban legend surrounding the game "Truth or Dare" often involves a malevolent spirit or entity that becomes attached to the game, forcing players to complete increasingly dangerous dares, sometimes resulting in deadly consequences if they refuse or fail to complete them; essentially, playing the game can invite a supernatural force that will punish players if they don't follow the rules of the game.

Truth or Dare – Official Game Rules

Objective

The goal of *Truth or Dare* is to have fun by answering personal questions truthfully or completing daring challenges.

Setup

- Gather at least **three or more players** in a circle.
- Decide on the **turn order** (e.g., clockwise rotation).
- Choose if there will be **any limitations** on truths or dares (e.g., no embarrassing public dares, no deeply personal questions, etc.).

How to Play

1. **A player is chosen to go first** (random selection or volunteer).
2. The chosen player picks another participant and asks:
    - **"Truth or Dare?"**
3. The selected player must choose:
    - **Truth** – They must answer a personal question honestly.
    - **Dare** – They must complete a challenge given by the asker.
4. If the player refuses to answer or complete the dare, they receive a **penalty** (decided by the group before playing, such as skipping a turn, doing a minor task, or taking a fun consequence).
5. After completing their turn, the player who was challenged selects the next person to ask, continuing the game.

Truth or Dare

Rules & Guidelines

- **Be respectful** – Avoid questions or dares that make others uncomfortable.
- **No backing out after choosing** – Once you pick "Truth" or "Dare," you must follow through.
- **Dares must be safe** – No harmful, dangerous, or illegal challenges.
- **No repeated questions** – Players cannot ask the same truth question twice in a row.
- **Players can set limits** – If someone has a boundary, respect it.
- **Group veto power** – If a dare is too extreme, the group can vote to modify it.

Optional Variations

- **Skip Option:** Each player gets **one free pass** to skip a truth or dare during the game.
- **Double Dare:** If a player refuses a dare, they can be given a *more difficult dare* instead.
- **Mystery Box:** Pre-write truths and dares on paper, and players draw one at random.

Ending the Game

The game ends when players agree to stop or set a time limit.

The urban myth surrounding *Truth or Dare* suggests that the game has **supernatural origins** and may be tied to **cursed or paranormal events**. Here are some of the most popular myths:

1. The Summoning Game Theory

Some believe that *Truth or Dare* is not just a party game but a disguised **summoning ritual**. The idea is that when people challenge each other to expose personal truths or complete reckless dares, they unknowingly open themselves to **spiritual manipulation**.

- According to legend, if someone refuses both **Truth** and **Dare**, a shadowy entity will choose a punishment for them.
- Some versions claim that an obscured presence (a "Game Master" or spirit) is always **watching and influencing** the game.

2. The Haunted Dare Myth

A common urban legend states that if you play *Truth or Dare* at **midnight**, especially on **Halloween** or during a **full moon**, the dares you complete may have **real consequences** beyond the game.

- One variation suggests that saying *"I refuse to play"* three times will anger a spirit, who will then curse the player.
- Some claim that a *"cursed dare"* can follow you into real life, making bad luck or strange occurrences happen afterward.

3. The Origin in an Ancient Ritual

Some myths suggest that *Truth or Dare* dates back to **medieval times** or **ancient pagan rituals**, where people were forced to confess secrets under threat of public humiliation or supernatural punishment.

- Some believe the game was originally part of **divination rituals**, where spirits would force players to tell the truth or complete a challenge to prove their loyalty.
- The phrase "truth or dare" might have once meant *"confess your sins or face the consequences."*

4. The Game That Never Ends

An eerie legend tells of a group of friends who played *Truth or Dare* but **never finished the game properly** (by declaring an official end).

- As a result, they were **haunted by mysterious events**, with dares appearing in their dreams or eerie whispers daring them to complete new challenges.

- The only way to stop the haunting was to **find the original group members and formally close the game together**—but by then, some had mysteriously disappeared.

5. The Cursed Game Incident

One of the scariest myths claims that a **specific version of the game** (often called **"The Devil's Truth or Dare"**) should never be played.

- The legend says that if you **light a candle, say "Truth or Dare?" to a mirror, and wait**—a shadowy figure will appear and force you to play.
- If you lie during a truth or fail a dare, the entity may **mark you** in some way (with a scratch, a whisper in the dark, or worse).

  NEVER, EVER, PLAY THIS GAME...

Patti Petrone Miller

TRUTH OR DARE

BE WARNED...

Truth or Dare

Authors Book List

Accidental Vows
A Very Merry Krampus Christmas
Sin Takes A Holiday
Barking Up The Wrong Bakery, Thankgiving
Barking Up The Wrong Bakery, Christmas
Best Served Dead
Bewitching Charms
Christmas at Hollybrook Inn
Christmas on Peppermit Lane
Cabinet of Curiosities
Krampus
Hex and the City
Love in Stitches
Pies and Perps
Spectres and Souffles
Mamma Mia It's Murder
Once Upon A Christmas
The Fatman
The Frosted Felony
The Purr-fect Suspect
The Boogeyman
The Gingerdead Men
Vikings Enchantress
Welcome to Scarecrow Hollow
The Pendleton Witches
The Cabinet of Curiosities
Christmas In Pine Haven
Love in the Stacks
Once Upon A Christmas
Frosted Felony
THE DEVIL OF LONDON

Reviews:

5.0 out of 5 stars

The Boogeyman is a Mind Blowing Ride into the Darkness!
Reviewed in the United States on March 7
The Boogeyman
Creepy in a fantastic way

The Boogeyman reads like the premise of a film noir. I could almost hear the ominous violins' warning crescendo in the background. Murray, the main character, is a young man plagued by nightmares. They have overtaken his life to the point where he is dependent on daily sessions with his psychiatrist just to keep from falling to pieces. The themes of repressed memories, murder and dangerous, almost experimental psychotherapy are not new but they are so enjoyable all the same. The Boogeyman employs a writing style that is superficial in quality, showing the reader scenes and characters that are familiar such as the loving mother that cooks gourmet feasts for all, the strong but silent father, and the good doctor. In my opinion, this was the perfect choice for this story because it allowed the feeling of paranoia to really seep through the cracks of the familiar backdrop. There were a few inconsistencies that could be my error for missing, for example, what did Murray end up getting his doting mother for Christmas? And how long had he lived in Boston? These, I must stress, could be my mistake and they did not at all distract from the enjoyment of the story. Grammar errors were few and it is overall very cleanly written. The Boogeyman is well paced, intriguing and delivers a fantastic story climax that is well worth the read.

THE BOOGEYMAN
Verified customer

I came across the opportunity to read and review The Boogeyman by Patti Petrone Miller from a group in Facebook. I was told that this book is in several schools and libraries and I was grateful my review was wanted after offering it.
This book held my attention from page one and it was packed full of thrills, terror, and spine tingling suspense for a short read. I was a little disappointed when it ended. I do have to confess but I thought I had it figured out from Chapter One and I am very seldom wrong because I have a talent in predicting the ending to movies and books with little knowledge of them, usually just from the first chapter in a book to the first 30 mins of a movie. So, I was very pleased when I discovered I was in fact wrong about the ending.
This book although in schools, I don't think it would be for small children. The author showed brilliance in describing the inside of the mind of his character when allowed to be altered by medications. The wonderful imagination of Miller set the stage for the reader to be pulled into the story therefore feeling the sheer terror of madness. I was able to feel what characters were feeling and going through, and sometimes it was a bit frightening. I loved it!!!
I highly recommend this book and give it five stars *****

Rosser's Relaxed Reviews
5 Stars

I have seven kids. That's right, count'em--one, two, three, four, five, six, seven. Do you know what that means? It means I've read just about every book written for people who haven't reached the age of majority. There's a weird dynamic. We start out reading books to them, like Andrew Lang's Fairy books and The Little Prince and Water Babies. Those are pretty fun. Then, they learn to read, so we're bored as heck watching and listening to them haltingly fight their ways through basic sentences. When they can read, most of what's available is complete junk. It isn't until Junior High or so that the kids reach an age where anyone is writing something they might actually enjoy.

And let's face it...ninety-nine percent of what's written for young adults is just crap. There, I said it. I'm serious, though. Most YA fiction isn't about the kids. It's written to a conglomerate vision of what we think the kids are. That's why every kid has the exact same challenges, hopes, and fears. That's why every kid falls in love the exact same way. That's why there's always one "goody two-shoes" character and one "bad" character. Really, the genre is so darn formulaic that you almost want to keep your kids illiterate until they can appreciate Hemingway Steinbeck, and Poe.

I'm happy to report that Patti Petrone Miller's book, The Boogeyman, doesn't fall into the trap. I liked it enough that it ended up a present for my twelve-year old to read. The book doesn't treat kids like feeble-minded idiots ready for emotional and intellectual manipulation. I really like that. It not only excites, but it provokes thought. Maybe I'm an old fashioned kind of parent, but I find it important that a book make my daughter think.

The characterization is excellent. I quite like the interactions between Murray and Doctor Rosen. I also like the psychological horror element of the book. It's a far cry from most YA horror which, if anything, pays only lip service to the psyche side of horror. I think it's remarkable that a young adult book focuses so much on older characters as well. You never see that.

The pacing is great. It starts slowly and builds with each chapter. The beginning could have been a little quicker, but there's no harm done. The twists are unexpected but they don't cheat the reader, and I was left wanting more, so I better see some more in the series, and I know my daughter will go on a Patti Petrone Miller hunt if she doesn't.

Pick the book up. it's a good one.

Patti Petrone Miller

For my little Beenie weenie weenie
Rest in Peace

Excerpt

Nathaniel's eyes flickered with something unreadable. "We're still playing."

Maria's voice was barely above a whisper. "Oh, hell no."

Nathaniel tilted his head, his smile widening as his fingers twitched erratically. "Your turn."

The house groaned, the floor vibrating beneath their feet. The walls began to *close in*, pressing inward, suffocating. The hallway distorted, stretching impossibly long in one moment before snapping back too close in the next.

Suddenly, the air crackled with energy, and a voice boomed from seemingly everywhere at once. "ENOUGH."

A surge of blinding white light split the darkness, and the shadows recoiled, shrieking as the temperature shifted abruptly. The sound of bells—low, rhythmic, pulsing—echoed through the walls, and then, stepping from the void, the witches emerged.

Miriam led them, her eyes burning with something otherworldly as she lifted her staff and struck it against the floor. The house *screamed*. "No more tricks," she hissed.

Miriam raised her hands, and the air seemed to *bend* around her as if reality itself were folding. "It's time to break your hold."

Nathaniel twitched violently, his smile turning into something *wrong*, his face contorting. "You don't belong here," he hissed.

Silas, standing just behind Miriam, whispered an incantation under his breath. A shimmering circle of symbols formed around the group, a barrier against the creeping darkness. "You have no power over them anymore," he declared.

The house *roared*, shaking its very foundation. The walls trembled, cracks forming in the ceiling. *It knew.* It *felt* the challenge.

A deep, guttural noise echoed from the farthest corners of the house, something ancient and *starving* waking within its walls. The whispers turned into screams, wailing in agony, clawing against the veil of reality the witches were pulling apart.

Elias turned to the girls. "Now. We finish this."

The game had just changed.

PROLOGUE: FIVE YEARS EARLIER

The Sinclair house loomed against the night sky, its silhouette jagged and unwelcoming. Shadows pooled in the hollows of its broken windows, and the porch steps sagged beneath decades of neglect. It was the kind of place that belonged in nightmares, not in the waking world of Millbrook—a town too small to hide its secrets, but somehow large enough to forget this decaying mansion on its outskirts.

Five figures moved through the overgrown yard, their flashlights bobbing like fireflies in the darkness. Sixteen years old and invincible, they laughed too loudly, their voices carrying through the still summer air.

"This is so stupid," Caroline muttered, tugging her blonde hair into a ponytail. Her designer jeans and pristine white sneakers looked painfully out of place against the wild tangle of weeds. "I can't believe I let you talk me into this."

Janey rolled her eyes, pushing ahead of the group. "It's just an old house, Car. Not everything has to be a drama."

"Says the girl who screamed when we watched 'The Ring,'" Rachel teased, her red hair glinting copper in the moonlight. She bumped Janey's shoulder playfully, the two of them leading the way as they always had since kindergarten.

Maria hung back slightly, her fingers fidgeting with the silver bracelet on her wrist. "My abuela says this place is cursed. That people who go in don't come out the same." Her voice was quiet, but it carried in the still night air.

Olivia scoffed, the perpetual skeptic. "Your abuela also thinks her cat can predict the weather." She flicked her flashlight beam across the house's facade. "It's just a house. A gross, moldy house that's probably full of rats and tetanus."

The porch steps creaked under their weight as they climbed, one by one, toward the front door. It hung partially open, as if in invitation—or warning.

"So what exactly are we doing here?" Maria asked, hesitating at the threshold.

Rachel grinned, producing a worn deck of cards from her backpack. "Truth or Dare. The Millbrook version." She waggled her eyebrows dramatically. "Legend says if you play in the Sinclair house, the stakes get... interesting."

"Interesting how?" Caroline's voice pitched higher.

"The house chooses the dares," Janey said, pushing the door open wider. The hinges protested with a sound like a wounded animal. "And it knows if you're lying."

"That's ridiculous," Olivia said, but her voice lacked its usual confidence.

Inside, the air was thick with dust and decay. Their flashlights cut through darkness that seemed too dense, revealing peeling wallpaper and floors warped with water damage. The house felt unnaturally cold despite the summer heat outside, as if winter had been trapped within its walls.

"Let's find a room that doesn't look like it'll collapse on us," Rachel suggested, leading them deeper into the house.

They settled in what must have once been a dining room. A heavy oak table dominated the space, surprisingly intact despite the house's overall deterioration. Scattered chairs surrounded it, their upholstery long rotted away.

"This is perfect," Rachel declared, placing the deck of cards in the center of the table. From her backpack, she also produced a white candle, which she set beside the cards.

"Seriously?" Caroline groaned. "Could you be more cliché?"

Rachel ignored her, striking a match and lighting the candle. The flame caught, casting their faces in shifting golden light. Shadows danced on the walls, stretching and contracting as if alive.

"Everyone sit," Rachel instructed. "And we need something to make this official."

"Like what?" Maria asked, reluctantly taking a seat.

Rachel thought for a moment, then pulled out a pocketknife. Before anyone could protest, she pricked her finger and let a single drop of blood fall onto the deck of cards.

"Jesus, Rachel!" Olivia exclaimed. "That's taking this way too far."

"It's just a drop," Rachel said with a shrug. "Now everyone has to do it."

"No way," Caroline protested, crossing her arms.

"Don't be such a baby," Janey said, taking the knife from Rachel. She winced slightly as she pricked her own finger, adding her blood to the deck. One by one, with varying degrees of reluctance, the others followed suit.

As the last drop—Maria's—touched the cards, the flame of the candle flickered violently. For a moment, it seemed to burn blue.

"Did you see that?" Maria whispered.

"It's just a draft," Olivia said firmly, but her eyes darted nervously to the shadowed corners of the room.

Rachel shuffled the deck, her movements practiced and precise. "The rules are simple. We take turns drawing cards. If you draw a heart or diamond, you choose truth. Spade or club, you take a dare. Refuse either, and... well, the house decides your punishment."

"That's not how Truth or Dare works," Caroline pointed out.

"It is here," Rachel replied, her voice taking on an odd quality. She placed the deck in the center of the table. "I'll go first."

She drew a card. The Queen of Spades.

"Dare," Rachel announced, her eyes gleaming in the candlelight.

The house seemed to hold its breath. The silence was absolute, pressing against their ears like cotton wool.

"This is stupid," Olivia began, but then stopped as the temperature in the room plummeted.

A whisper slithered through the air, so soft they almost missed it.

Go to the basement door. Open it. Count to thirteen.

Rachel's face paled. "Did you hear that?"

The others nodded, wide-eyed.

"I'm not doing that," Rachel said, forcing a laugh. "This is just some kind of mass hallucination or—"

The candle flame shot upward, nearly reaching the ceiling. The table beneath their hands vibrated, and a low groan emanated from the walls around them.

"Okay! Okay," Rachel said quickly. "I'll do it."

She stood, her legs visibly shaking. The others followed as she made her way through the house, guided by some invisible knowledge of where the basement door was located.

They found it at the end of a narrow hallway—a simple wooden door with a tarnished brass knob. It looked innocuous enough, but as they approached, Maria let out a whimper.

"Something's not right," she whispered. "Can't you feel it?"

Rachel reached for the doorknob, hesitated, then pulled her hand back. "I can't," she admitted. "I just... I can't."

The house responded immediately. The floor beneath them tilted sharply, sending them all stumbling. The walls seemed to contract, the hallway narrowing impossibly. A cold wind whipped through the corridor, carrying whispers too fast and numerous to understand.

"Do it!" Caroline screamed, grabbing the wall for support. "Just do it!"

Rachel lunged for the knob, twisted it, and wrenched the door open.

Darkness. Absolute and complete. Not the darkness of an unlit room, but something deeper, hungrier. Something alive.

"One," Rachel began counting, her voice shaking. "Two..."

A sound emerged from the darkness below. Something moving. Something heavy.

"Three... four... five..."

The walls continued to contract. The house was breathing, pulsing around them.

"Six... seven... eight..."

A smell rose from the basement—decay and rot and something metallic, like old blood.

"Nine... ten..."

The whispering intensified, a frantic chorus of voices begging, pleading.

"Eleven... twelve..."

Something reached the bottom step. They couldn't see it, but they could sense it—a presence, massive and ancient.

"Thirteen!"

Rachel slammed the door shut just as something struck the other side with incredible force. The impact reverberated through the house like a gunshot.

They ran, stumbling over each other in their haste to escape. Behind them, doors began slamming open and shut on their own. The wooden floor buckled and heaved as if the house itself was convulsing.

"Keep going!" Janey shouted, pushing Caroline ahead of her as they reached the main hall.

They burst through the front door into the cool night air, gasping and trembling. But they didn't stop. They ran until the house was out of sight, until they reached the safety of streetlights and paved roads.

Finally, at the edge of town, they collapsed onto the grass of the community park, gulping in air that didn't taste of dust and fear.

"What... the hell... was that?" Olivia panted, her earlier skepticism evaporated.

"We need to go back," Rachel said suddenly.

They all stared at her in disbelief.

"Are you insane?" Caroline shrieked.

"The game," Rachel insisted. "We didn't finish it. We left the cards, the candle. We left the game unfinished."

"So what?" Janey asked, but there was uncertainty in her voice. She knew, somehow, that Rachel was right.

"That's not how it works," Maria said quietly. "You have to end the game properly. You have to say goodbye."

A chill ran through them that had nothing to do with the night air.

"It's fine," Olivia said firmly. "It was just an old house playing tricks on our minds. Mass hysteria or whatever."

"Then why are you shaking?" Janey asked.

Olivia had no answer.

"We'll go back tomorrow," Rachel decided. "In daylight. We'll end the game properly, and that will be that."

But they didn't go back the next day. Or the day after. The summer slipped away, and with it, their resolve. School started, and the Sinclair house became a story they told at sleepovers, a secret that bound them together.

They convinced themselves it had been nothing—just their imaginations, fueled by local legends and Rachel's flair for the dramatic. They almost believed it.

Until the dreams began.

The same dream, night after night. The five of them, back in the dining room of the Sinclair house. The cards. The candle. The game continuing without them, waiting for their return.

And a voice, patient and terrible, whispering from the shadows:

Your turn.

For five years, they ignored it. For five years, they pretended not to hear.

But the game wasn't over.

And now, it wanted to play again.

The wind howled against the abandoned house, rattling the loose windowpanes like shrouded fingers demanding entry. The town of Millbrook was asleep, oblivious to the four women standing in the entryway of the old Sinclair residence. Dust swirled in the dim glow of Janey's flashlight, dancing like restless ghosts in the stale air. The bitter scent of damp wood and mildew filled their nostrils, mingling with the underlying coppery tang of something else—something they didn't want to acknowledge.

Each of them had changed over the past five years, yet standing here, in front of the house that had stolen their peace, they felt sixteen again—foolish, invincible, and utterly unprepared for what lurked in the shadows. The memories clung to them, ghostly fingers tracing the nape of their necks, whispering in voices only they could hear.

Janey, the anchor of the group, had always been the one to push forward, to suppress fear in the name of reason. Her hazel eyes, sharp and assessing, scanned the peeling wallpaper and warped wooden floors. She had a naturally serious expression, one that had deepened with time. Her auburn hair was pulled into a messy bun, wisps framing her high cheekbones. Dressed in a fitted leather jacket and jeans, she looked ready for battle, though the tremble in her fingers betrayed her unease.

A shiver ran down Caroline's spine as she hugged herself. The air in the house seemed wrong. "This was a fucking mistake," she muttered, her voice brittle.

Caroline was the smallest of them, but what she lacked in height, she made up for in attitude. Her wavy blonde hair, usually styled to perfection, was now windblown and tangled. Her blue eyes darted from shadow to shadow, tracking the whatever she saw. She had always been the most vocal about her fears, the most reluctant, yet here she was, standing among them, drawn back by the same haunting force that plagued her dreams.

Janey ignored her, stepping forward cautiously. Her boots scuffed against the warped wooden floors, each step loud in the suffocating silence. "We said we'd do this," she reminded them, her voice steadier than she felt. "We left the game unfinished. It's time we finish it."

Olivia clicked her tongue, unimpressed. "It's been five years, Janey. No one cares about a stupid game of Truth or Dare anymore."

Olivia had always been the fearless one, or at least, that was the persona she projected. Her dark, shoulder-length hair fell in loose waves around her sharp features, and her deep brown eyes gleamed with something unreadable. She wore a sleek black trench coat, her lips painted blood red. She looked unaffected, but Janey saw the way her fingers twitched slightly, the way her breath was just a little too measured.

Maria exhaled a shaky breath, her hands gripping the straps of her purse like a lifeline. "Then why do we all still have the same nightmares?"

Maria, always the mediator, had a softness to her. Her deep olive skin glowed in the dim light, and her curly brown hair was tucked into a low ponytail. She smelled faintly of vanilla and chamomile, a stark contrast to the dust and decay around them. Of all of them, she had been the most hesitant to return, but she had agreed. Because she knew, just like they all did, that something was unfinished here.

The group fell silent. The nightmares. The whispers in the dark. The shadows that never quite felt like their own.

Rachel, standing slightly apart from the group, glanced over her shoulder at the empty street. The town had always been too quiet at night, but now, the silence was unnatural. Like the world beyond the house didn't exist anymore. She swallowed hard. "Let's just get this over with."

Rachel was the tallest, her slender frame tense with barely contained energy. Her red hair, once vibrant, had dulled slightly over the years. She was dressed in an oversized sweater and leggings, her fingers gripping the sleeves as if she could physically shield herself from whatever was coming.

Janey turned and stepped deeper into the house. The walls were lined with peeling wallpaper, floral patterns faded and curling at the edges. The air smelled of mold, old wood, and something faintly metallic. She reached the dining room— the place where it all started.

The table was still there, covered in a thick layer of dust. The candle they had burned that night had melted into a puddle, wax hardened into grotesque shapes. A deck of playing cards lay scattered across the surface, the edges warped from moisture, the red suits faded to a sickly brown.

The wind outside roared, hammering against the walls as if it wanted in. A deep creak echoed through the house, a slow, deliberate noise that sent ice down Janey's spine. Dust shifted on the shelves, a fine trickle cascading onto the table.

Rachel clenched her fists. "This isn't funny."

"Who the fuck is laughing?" Olivia snapped, her bravado faltering.

A sudden bang erupted from upstairs.

The women froze. Caroline whimpered, covering her mouth with trembling fingers. Janey's breath hitched, her eyes darting toward the staircase. The sound hadn't been random. It had weight, purpose.

Maria exhaled slowly. "We... we should leave."

But the front door was already closed. The moment they had stepped inside, it had sealed behind them, locking them into the past they had tried so hard to forget.

Then, without warning, the candle on the table flickered, stretching unnaturally high, casting sharp, dancing shadows across the walls. And as they stood there, frozen, a single card slid across the table on its own.

Rachel jumped back with a sharp gasp. "No. Fuck that."

Caroline's breath hitched in her throat. "Tell me someone else saw that."

Maria took a shaky step forward, staring at the card. The Ace of Spades. Her voice was barely above a whisper. "It's starting."

The shadows seemed to pulse, moving as if breathing, stretching and twisting. The house was waking up.

And it was hungry.

Two

The candle on the dust-covered table flickered violently, as though something had exhaled over it. The air inside the Sinclair house thickened, carrying the faint, metallic scent of rust—of blood. The women stood frozen, their gazes locked on the Ace of Spades that had just moved on its own.

Janey inhaled sharply, forcing herself to remain grounded. "It's just a draft," she murmured, though her voice lacked conviction.

"No, it's not," Caroline shot back, arms wrapped tightly around herself. Her blue eyes darted from shadow to shadow, her breath shallow. "Something is here."

Rachel exhaled a slow, trembling breath, her fingers twitching at her sides. "We knew what we were walking into."

Maria took a hesitant step forward, her gaze locked on the card. The edges of it curled slightly, as if it had been exposed to heat. "We left the game unfinished."

A gust of wind slammed the door behind them, sending dust spiraling in frantic patterns. Olivia jumped, her bravado slipping for the first time. "That wasn't the wind."

Janey forced herself to speak, to think logically. "We need to finish what we started." She stepped toward the table, her fingers hovering over the warped deck. "If this house is holding onto something, maybe this is the only way to get rid of it."

Maria shuddered but nodded. "We ask the next question."

Olivia swallowed hard. "Fine. But I'm not picking a damn card."

Rachel's fingers hesitated before she reached out and drew one from the deck. The moment she flipped it over, the room seemed to tilt slightly, the air thick with energy.

King of Hearts.

A sharp whisper slithered through the room, brushing against their ears, indistinct yet intimate. The candle's flame elongated unnaturally, stretching higher, casting grotesque shadows that writhed across the peeling wallpaper.

Caroline's voice was barely above a whisper. "What does it mean?"

Rachel's hands trembled as she placed the card on the table. "Truth or Dare," she murmured.

The house answered.

A loud *thump* echoed from the second floor.

All the women flinched, their heads snapping upward.

Janey's mouth went dry. "It wants us to choose."

Maria took a step back, her spine pressing against the wall. "We shouldn't."

Rachel's throat bobbed with a swallow, her gaze darting to each of them before settling on Janey. "Truth."

The whisper came again, curling through the air like a breath against their skin. But this time, it spoke. A voice, hollow and distant, yet terribly familiar.

"What happened the night of the fire?"

Caroline gasped. Maria let out a sharp breath.

Rachel's stomach twisted. Her lips parted, but no words came.

"I—"

The candle flickered violently, sending twisted shadows lurching across the walls. A sudden pressure built in the room, heavy, oppressive. The evil force was waiting.

Rachel's hands clenched into fists. She hadn't spoken of that night since they had all fled town. Not to the police. Not to her therapist. Not to herself.

"We didn't start it." Her voice cracked. "But we didn't stop it, either."

The room groaned, the walls seeming to shift. The scent of smoke curled in the air—thick, suffocating. A cruel reminder of the past they had buried.

The whisper returned, colder this time. "Liar."

The candle extinguished, plunging them into darkness.

Caroline whimpered. Olivia cursed under her breath. Maria grabbed for Janey's arm, her fingers like ice.

Then, footsteps. Slow. Deliberate. Coming from upstairs.

Janey's breath caught. "We're not alone."

The air turned frigid as the footsteps grew closer, descending the staircase with an agonizing slowness. Each creak of the old wood sent a jolt of fear down Janey's spine.

The shadows shifted.

A shape loomed at the top of the stairs.

Rachel sucked in a sharp breath. "It's him."

The candle flared back to life, revealing an empty staircase.

But the game wasn't over.

The next card slid forward on its own.

Queen of Spades.

A piercing scream echoed through the house, but none of them had made a sound. The floor beneath them vibrated as if something massive stirred beneath the rotting wood. The air thickened with an oppressive weight, pressing against their chests.

Olivia staggered back, clutching her stomach. "I—I don't want to do this anymore."

Maria shook her head, her curls sticking to her sweat-slicked forehead. "We can't stop."

Caroline's breathing turned ragged as she pressed against the wall. "The house won't let us."

The wallpaper near the staircase began to curl, peeling away to reveal something underneath. Not wood. Not plaster.

Flesh.

Dark veins ran beneath the surface, pulsing in time with the steady thud of something moving below them. The scent of rot and burning hair filled the air.

Rachel's knees buckled, and she clapped a hand over her mouth. "Oh God."

The candle's flame stretched unnaturally again, twisting in the air like reaching fingers.

A whisper, right behind Janey's ear, sent ice through her veins. "Choose wisely."

A new card flipped onto the table by itself. The Joker.

The floor trembled. A deep, guttural chuckle rumbled through the walls, the sound soaked in something ancient and malevolent.

Janey forced herself to look at the others, their faces pale, their eyes wide with unspeakable fear.

This wasn't just a game anymore.

It never had been.

THREE

The candle on the table flared once more, but the light it cast was wrong. The flame twisted unnaturally, writhing like a living thing, stretching toward the ceiling as though hands clawed at it. The girls stood in frozen silence, their breath uneven, their bodies tense. The air inside the Sinclair house had thickened, weighted with something evil, something watching. The walls, the very floor beneath them, seemed to inhale and exhale in slow, deliberate intervals, as if waiting.

Then, a whisper. Not from the shadows, not from the creaking walls, but from the Joker card resting on the table. The voice slithered around them, curling into their ears like a secret.

"Who's next?"

Caroline whimpered, her fingers digging into Maria's arm with enough force to leave bruises. "This isn't happening. It's just in our heads."

Janey—logical, skeptical Janey—couldn't pretend anymore. The way the air clung to her skin like damp cloth, the way the candle's flame burned black at its edges, told her otherwise. She swallowed hard, her voice shaking. "We keep playing."

Olivia let out a sharp, humorless laugh. "Are you insane? The house—it's—it's breathing."

And it was. A deep, rhythmic groan echoed through the floorboards, a pulsing sound, slow and deliberate. The wallpaper continued to peel, revealing something that wasn't wood or plaster underneath—something that pulsed, dark veins stretching under the surface. The Joker card twitched, then spun in slow circles before landing face up.

Rachel's breath hitched. "It's picking for us."

The candle dimmed. The shadows thickened, stretching, reaching. The voice came again, a whisper tangled in static. "Truth... or dare?"

Maria sucked in a breath, her voice barely above a whisper. "Truth."

A violent gust of wind slammed against the windows, rattling the broken panes like frantic fingers scraping to get inside. The whisper turned guttural, its syllables dripping with malice. "What do you dream about?"

Maria stiffened, her lips parting as if the words had been stolen from her lungs. Her pulse pounded, her skin clammy with sweat.

"I—" she swallowed hard, her wide eyes darting to the others. "I dream about fire."

The walls groaned. The acrid scent of smoke slithered through the air, thick and choking, curling into their noses like burning flesh. Something shifted above them, slow and deliberate, as if responding to her words.

Rachel gasped. "Don't answer it—"

Maria's voice cracked. "I see us. The four of us. Trapped in this house. Burning."

A moan, low and ragged, rumbled from above. The ceiling beams groaned, bowing under a weight, dust sifting down in lazy spirals. The candle flickered, throwing their shadows across the walls—long, distorted, monstrous versions of themselves, moving even when they didn't.

Then, silence. Suffocating, oppressive. The only sound was the unsteady breathing of the women.

Janey moved first. She snatched the Joker card and hurled it across the room. "No more," she snapped, her voice cracking. "We end this now."

A dry, rasping chuckle rolled through the walls.

The table bucked beneath their hands.

Not a subtle shake. Not the slow groan of aged wood shifting. It lurched violently, sending the deck of cards spiraling into the air, hanging there as if caught in invisable hands before drifting down like leaves in water.

And the Joker card was back.

Face up.

A door upstairs slammed so hard the walls trembled. Heavy, deliberate footsteps followed, descending the staircase with unbearable slowness. Each step sent a vibration through the house, the weight of something immense pressing into the wood.

The shadows on the stairs lengthened before the figure came into view.

Rachel inhaled sharply, her fingernails biting into her palms.

A man stood at the bottom of the stairs.

But he wasn't a man.

His limbs were wrong—too long, too thin, his fingers ending in charred, jagged tips like burnt bone. His face was an ever-shifting blur, like a smear in reality itself, flickering between expressions that didn't belong to him. But his mouth

—that was constant. A grin, too wide for his face, filled with teeth like shattered glass.

"Your turn," he said, his voice the same whisper that had haunted them all night.

Caroline let out a sob, her back pressing against the wall. "We need to run."

Maria shook her head, her breaths shallow. "We can't."

The figure took a step forward, and the lights flickered wildly. The floor beneath them groaned, sinking slightly, as if something vast stirred beneath the house. The shadows began to crawl, stretching up the walls, clinging to their skin.

Janey forced herself to move. "Dare," she choked out, her heart hammering against her ribs.

The whisper curled through the air, laced with laughter. "I dare you… to open the basement door."

Silence. Even the house seemed to hold its breath.

Janey's eyes flickered to the hallway. The basement door stood slightly ajar, a sliver of blackness beyond it. A draft coiled out from the gap, thick and wet, carrying the scent of decay.

Rachel grabbed Janey's wrist. "Don't."

The figure at the foot of the stairs tilted its head, watching. Waiting. The candlelight made its grin gleam.

Janey pulled free. "If I don't do it, it'll make us."

She took a step forward. Then another. The air turned viscous, clinging to her skin, dragging at her clothes. The others whispered frantic protests behind her, but she didn't stop. She couldn't.

Her fingers curled around the basement doorknob. It was ice-cold.

She pushed it open.

The darkness beyond wasn't empty.

It moved.

A breath, slow and deep, exhaled from the void, carrying something wet and rotten with it.
A scream erupted from the abyss.
Something lunged.
And the candle went out.

FOUR

Darkness swallowed them whole. The scream that erupted from the basement wasn't just sound—it was pressure, a force that rattled their bones and sent a wave of nausea curling in their stomachs. The air was thick with something vile, an wicked presence that slithered around them, whispering just beneath the threshold of understanding.

Janey staggered back, her hands clawing at the doorframe as if she could physically push the darkness away. "Close it! Close it now!" she shrieked, her voice a strangled cry.

But she couldn't move. None of them could.

Rachel's breath hitched, her hands frozen inches from the door. "I… I can't."

The shadows around them pulsed, shifting with sickening fluidity. A slow, heavy *thud* came from the basement, followed by another. Then another. Footsteps, but not human ones—too heavy, too wet, dragging against the wooden steps like something covered in thick sludge. The scent of rot intensified, stinging their nostrils and coating their tongues with decay.

Maria let out a choked sob. "It's coming."

The candle on the table, long extinguished, flared back to life in an instant, its flame burning blue. A harsh, guttural whisper wrapped around them. "You chose. Now play."

The basement door wrenched open violently, splintering against the wall. The air turned freezing. The room twisted. The walls seemed to stretch, elongating as if the house itself were expanding into something unnatural.

Then, something crawled out.

It moved in jagged, spasmodic lurches, as if it wasn't meant to exist in this world. Its body was long, impossibly thin, its skin stretched tight like old parchment over protruding bones. Its head… there was no face, only a shifting blur, like static on a dead television screen. Its arms—too many of them—unfurled, clawing at the floor, the walls, reaching.

Caroline screamed and bolted toward the door, but the house refused to let her go. The doorknob twisted violently in place, rattling as if something on the other side was holding it shut.

Rachel shoved past Janey, snatching up the deck of cards scattered across the table. "It's the game! We have to finish it!" she shouted. "That's the only way out!"

Olivia turned, her face pale, sweat slicking her forehead. "We don't know that!"

A guttural, wet clicking sound came from the creature, as if it was laughing.

The table jerked, sending the cards flying. One landed face-up. The Queen of Hearts.

A silence stretched across the room before a deep, unnatural *thud* shook the walls.

Another voice slithered through the air.

"Who bleeds first?"

Janey's stomach plummeted. The walls pulsed. The creature crept forward.

The game wasn't over.

And now, it wanted more than just their fear.

Maria's hands clenched into fists, her breathing ragged as she fought against the sheer panic threatening to consume her. "We have to be smart. It's waiting for us to panic."

Caroline wiped sweat from her brow with trembling fingers. "Smart? We're trapped in a nightmare! I'm done playing its game."

Rachel kept her gaze locked on the flickering candle. "If we don't play, it will force us."

Janey sucked in a shaky breath, trying to steady her thoughts. "Fine. But we play on our terms."

The creature remained motionless, its fingers twitching against the wooden floor. The whisper returned, taunting. "One of you must pay."

Rachel scanned the scattered deck, searching for patterns. "It's not random. There's a method to this."

The cards shuffled themselves in an eerie, fluid motion, a single card sliding forward. The Jack of Diamonds.

The room held its breath.

A sharp, metallic *click* echoed through the air, and a blade materialized on the table—gleaming, impossibly thin.

Janey exhaled sharply, her hands shaking. "Blood. That's what it wants."

Maria swallowed hard, forcing logic through her fear. "Not necessarily death. Just... blood."

Janey hesitated, then pressed the blade to her finger, a single crimson drop welling before hitting the wood.

The house shuddered.

The creature let out a satisfied hiss, retracting into the shadows, its form dissolving like smoke.

A deep exhale echoed through the walls, the foundation trembling. The cards shifted, snapping into a neat pile. Another slid forward.

The Ace of Spades.

"The price has been paid… for now," the voice murmured, distant yet ever-present.

The floor beneath them groaned, something massive shifting below. A chuckle drifted from the basement.

The game continued.

A rush of air whipped through the room, sending dust and brittle fragments of paper swirling into the candle's weak glow. The sound of rattling chains echoed from beneath the floorboards, a hollow, rattling whisper that sent icy tendrils creeping up Janey's spine.

"Do you feel that?" Olivia's voice barely registered above a whisper, her hands trembling as she reached for the deck.

Rachel narrowed her eyes, scanning the room for any sign of movement. "The house is reacting. It knows we're fighting back."

Caroline clenched her jaw, trying to steady her fraying nerves. "Then we fight smarter."

The Queen of Hearts lay abandoned on the table, its edges curling and darkening as if charred from within. The whisper returned, slithering against the back of their skulls, winding into their ears like smoke.

"Play your next card."

Rachel inhaled sharply and reached for the deck, her fingers brushing against the worn edges. The second she touched it, the candle's flame shuddered, flaring high before extinguishing completely.

Blackness consumed them.

Then, something *moved*.

A scrape, slow and deliberate, against the wooden floor.

Janey held her breath, gripping the edge of the table so tightly her knuckles turned white. A whisper, closer this time, slithered through the void. "Choose wisely."

The air was thick, suffocating. A new card slid forward, its surface glinting in the dark.

Rachel fumbled for a match, her fingers slick with sweat. She struck it, the tiny flame revealing the card's face.

The King of Spades.

The floor trembled. A gust of wind howled through the room, rattling the windows. The creature shifted in the darkness, waiting.

Caroline swallowed hard. "What does that mean?"

The whisper came again, a sinister chuckle laced in its tone. "The king takes his throne."

The walls shuddered, deep groans resonating from within them. Something else was coming.

Something worse.

Five

A low, guttural growl reverberated through the house, deeper than the whispers that had plagued them before. This was different. Heavier. A presence that had always been lurking but now stood at the edge of revelation. The King had made his move.

The moment the King of Spades was revealed, the temperature in the room dropped sharply, their breath curling into mist in the oppressive dark. The candle, the only source of light, flared wildly before extinguishing completely. An unnatural silence followed, thick and choking, pressing against their ears like the weight of demonic hands.

Then came the sound.

A scraping. Slow, deliberate, dragging against the wooden floor. It echoed from all directions, circling them, as though something massive was shifting within the walls, moving between the beams and plaster like a shadow slipping through cracks.

Caroline let out a shaky breath, backing toward the table. "What does it want now?"

Rachel's hands trembled as she reached for the deck again, her fingers brushing against the cards' worn edges. "We have to stay ahead of it," she murmured. "The game isn't over. We need to play."

Janey swallowed hard, her mind racing. The King had been drawn. That had to mean something, something more than just another cruel trick.

A gust of wind rattled the windows. Then, a voice.

"Bow before your King."

It wasn't a whisper. It was a demand.

The floor beneath them trembled, dust spiraling upward as the air itself seemed to vibrate with the force of the words. Maria let out a strangled gasp, clutching at her chest as though something had tightened around her lungs.

"We don't bow to anything!" Olivia shouted, her voice raw with defiance, but there was an unmistakable quiver in it.

A laugh—low, amused, ancient—rippled through the house.

The darkness shifted. And then they saw it.

A figure stood at the far end of the room, where the walls met the void, its form half-consumed by the abyss. It was tall—too tall—its limbs stretched beyond what should be humanly possible. Its head tilted, the static distortion of its face flickering in and out of focus, revealing glimpses of something far worse beneath. The grin, wide and jagged, was the only thing that remained consistent.

The King.

Janey's pulse thundered. "What do we do?" she whispered.

The King took a step forward. The floor groaned in protest beneath its weight. It did not hurry. It did not need to.

The game had only just begun.

Rachel's mind raced. There had to be a pattern, a way to outmaneuver whatever rules the house was forcing upon them.

If they played incorrectly, the consequences would be irreversible.

"We draw again," she said, her voice barely audible. "We keep going. We don't let it take control."

The others hesitated, but Maria nodded first, her expression grim. "Then let's play."

Another card slid forward from the deck on its own.

The House always played first.

The card spun slowly as if caught in a current, twisting in the stale air before landing face-up in the center of the table. The Jack of Clubs.

Rachel's fingers twitched at her sides, her breathing shallow. "What does that mean?"

A soft tapping sound filled the room. It started as a distant rhythm, a light *tap tap tap* against the floorboards. Then it grew louder, closer. The source was ghostly, but the cadence was methodical, precise—as if something was counting down.

Maria turned her head sharply, her pulse racing. "It's waiting for us to act."

Caroline took a cautious step forward, eyeing the card as though it might lunge at her. "If the King rules, what does the Jack do?"

The King's grin widened. The distorted static of his face flickered violently as the tapping escalated into a pounding— *boom boom boom*—each pulse of sound rattling the windows, the walls, the very air around them.

A door slammed somewhere in the house. Then another. And another. The house was shifting, closing in, rearranging itself into something unfamiliar.

Janey turned sharply, her voice edged with desperation. "It's forcing us to move. We have to make a choice."

The deck shuddered. Another card pushed itself forward.

The Queen of Diamonds.

The King let out a low, rumbling growl that vibrated through their bones. The temperature plummeted again, the floor beneath them slick with ice that hadn't been there moments before. Their breaths came in short, visible puffs, but none of them dared to move.

Rachel grabbed Olivia's arm, her nails digging into the fabric of her shirt. "I don't think we can play our way out of this."

The King took another step forward, and the world seemed to contract around him. Shadows twisted, bending in ways that defied reality. His elongated fingers flexed, the bones cracking with each movement. The grin stretched impossibly wide, the edges of his mouth curling back into something more akin to a wound than a smile.

"You misunderstand," the voice slithered through the darkness, wrapping around them like a noose. "This is not your game to win."

The lights flickered wildly before exploding into shards of glass, raining down on them. The house roared, the walls vibrating with an demonic force. The shadows no longer stayed in place—they moved freely now, slithering like liquid smoke, reaching, grasping.

Caroline gasped, stumbling backward. "Then what are we supposed to do?!"

The King stopped. The house quieted.

The answer came in a whisper so close, so intimate, it was as if the words had been breathed directly into their ears.

"Survive."

Then, all at once, the floor collapsed beneath them.

They plunged downward, weightless, into a darkness that did not welcome them but consumed them whole. Air rushed past their ears, a void swallowing every scream before it could fully form. The sensation of falling stretched unnaturally, as though the space they had been thrown into had no bottom, no end.

Then—impact.

Janey hit the ground hard, pain radiating through her limbs. Dust and debris rained down as she gasped for breath, her fingers scrambling against cold stone. The others landed around her, groaning in shock, bodies sprawled in a heap on the unyielding floor.

A dim, flickering light revealed walls of damp stone, slick with moisture. The air smelled of mildew and decay, ancient and untouched. Chains clanked somewhere in the distance, and the unmistakable sound of breathing—slow, measured, inhuman—filled the space.

Maria forced herself upright, wincing. "Where are we?"

Rachel turned in a slow circle, her heart pounding. "Not in the house anymore."

A rasping exhale echoed from the shadows. Then a voice, deeper than before, impossibly close.

"The game continues. And now, the real fun begins."

The darkness surged forward, curling around them like a living thing, whispering promises of horrors yet to come. Walls of stone shuddered with forces pressing in as the stale air thickened with shadowed movements. From the depths of the void, something else stirred.

A second voice—hollow, echoing—laughed softly.

"Shall we raise the stakes?"

A set of ancient iron doors creaked open behind them, revealing an abyss lined with flickering torches, each flame burning an unnatural shade of blue. The stone floor beneath their feet groaned as though something immense shifted just below the surface, waiting.

SIX

The moment the iron doors groaned open, the torches lining the walls flared violently, their eerie blue flames licking at the stone like hungry specters. The air inside was thick, damp, reeking of earth and something far worse—something old, metallic, and cloying. Blood.

Janey steadied herself against the uneven ground, her fingers brushing over damp moss that clung to the walls like rotting flesh. The stone beneath her palms pulsed with a slow, rhythmic vibration, as if the place itself was alive, breathing in sync with their racing hearts.

"I don't want to go in there," Caroline whispered, her voice fragile, barely audible above the flickering torches. Her arms wrapped tightly around herself, shoulders trembling. "Whatever's waiting—it wants us to step inside. It's luring us."

Rachel's jaw clenched, her gaze locked on the archway leading into the abyss. "We don't have a choice. If we stay out here, it'll come for us. At least in there, we can see what's coming."

A sound slithered through the corridor ahead—wet, deliberate, like something dragging itself through stagnant water. The low ceiling seemed to press down, constricting the air, thickening it with every passing second.

Maria exhaled shakily. "Then we move together. No splitting up. No second-guessing. We keep moving no matter what."

Olivia swallowed hard, then nodded. "Agreed."

They stepped forward in unison, crossing the threshold beneath the ancient archway. The moment the last of them entered, the doors slammed shut behind them with a deafening *boom*, sending a pulse through the air that rattled their bones.

Darkness.

Then, a voice—low, guttural, and far too close.

"Welcome to the next round."

The torches along the corridor flared once more, casting grotesque shadows along the damp walls. The passage ahead stretched forward into an unnatural vastness, curving in ways that defied logic. Shapes flickered at the edges of the light, moving just beyond sight—watching.

A slow drip echoed from somewhere above, rhythmic and steady, like a ticking clock counting down to something inevitable. With every step, the stone beneath their feet shifted, groaning as if bearing an immense weight. The walls, slick with condensation, pulsed ever so slightly, like the throat of some massive beast.

Maria tightened her grip on Rachel's wrist. "Keep your eyes forward. Don't look at the walls. Don't listen. Just move."

They pressed on, feet shuffling cautiously over uneven ground. The air grew colder, wrapping around them like icy tendrils. The shadows stretched, twisted, moving independently of the flickering torchlight. Then came the whispering.

Not from ahead.

Not from behind.

From *inside* the walls.

Janey froze, her breath catching. "You hear that?"

Rachel nodded slowly, scanning the corridor. "They're talking."

The voices seeped from the cracks between the stones, distant yet familiar, layering over one another in an unholy chorus.

"Why did you leave me?"

"You said you'd help me."

"I called your name. Why didn't you answer?"

Caroline whimpered, pressing her hands against her ears. "Don't listen. It's not real."

Maria gritted her teeth, forcing herself to focus on the path ahead. "Keep moving. Don't answer them."

The whispers grew louder, overlapping, suffocating. Shadows spilled onto the ground like ink, swirling around their ankles, gripping their feet as if to anchor them in place. The corridor twisted again, stretching impossibly long, the exit nowhere in sight.

Then, the torches dimmed, and the whispering ceased.

Silence.

The space around them seemed to hold its breath. Then, a single word echoed through the corridor, spoken in a voice that was not their own.

"Run."

A deafening *roar* erupted from behind them. The shadows surged, coalescing into something massive, something with claws, with teeth—something that had been waiting.

Maria didn't think. She grabbed Rachel's arm and yanked her forward. "Go!"

They sprinted, feet pounding against the stone, the passage warping around them as they ran. The walls *moved*, shifting in ways they shouldn't, corridors splitting and reforming, leading them in circles. The air grew thick, dense, suffocating.

Behind them, the thing was gaining.

Janey stole a glance over her shoulder—and immediately wished she hadn't.

It was *fast*. A writhing mass of shifting limbs, too many eyes, its mouth stretching open *too wide*, revealing rows of jagged, glistening teeth. It didn't run—it *crawled*, pulling itself forward in sick, unnatural lurches, closing the distance far too quickly.

"LEFT!" Olivia screamed.

They veered sharply into a branching corridor just as something *slammed* into the ground where they had been, sending cracks splintering through the stone. The impact shook the walls, dust raining from the ceiling as the beast let out a piercing screech.

The corridor ahead narrowed, twisting in unnatural angles. The torches barely flickered now, their blue light sputtering, struggling to survive.

Rachel gasped for breath, her lungs burning. "Where's the exit?!"

"There isn't one!" Caroline cried. "We're trapped!"

Then, up ahead, something shifted—a sliver of light, faint, flickering through an arched doorway. An escape?

Maria's heart pounded as she pushed herself faster. "There! Keep going!"

They reached the threshold just as the creature *lunged*. The impact sent a wave of force through the passage, flinging them forward, crashing through the archway and tumbling into another chamber. The moment they crossed the threshold, the door behind them *vanished*—no stone, no exit, just solid wall.

The beast was gone.

Silence.

Panting, Maria pushed herself up, shaking. "Everyone okay?"

Rachel coughed, dusting debris off her arms. "Still alive."

Janey groaned, rubbing her shoulder. "Where *are* we now?"

They turned slowly, taking in their surroundings. The chamber was circular, lined with aged, crumbling bookshelves. Symbols, ancient and foreboding, were etched into the walls, glowing faintly with an unnatural blue light. At the room's center stood a table, and upon it—another deck of cards.

A voice—calm, patient—broke the silence.

"Shuffle, and we'll begin the next round."

The torches flared.

The game wasn't over.

From the shadows above, a quiet *click* echoed through the chamber, followed by another. Something was shifting—watching. The weight of watchful eyes pressed down on them as if the room itself was studying its players, calculating their fear.

Caroline stepped back from the table, her breath shallow. "This isn't a game anymore. It never was."

A slow, deliberate chuckle seeped through the walls, chilling them to their core.

"Oh, but it is. And now... the stakes are much higher."

The cards shuffled themselves.

The torches flickered again, casting elongated, dancing shadows along the walls. A deep, resounding *boom* reverberated through the chamber as maleviolent forces locked them in. The walls quivered, as if anticipating the next move.

Then, as if commanded by something, the deck of cards lifted from the table, hovering mid-air. One by one, the cards fanned out, their edges glowing with an eerie luminescence.

The voice spoke again, silkier this time, dripping with amusement.

"It's your turn to deal. Choose wisely."

Then, the first card turned itself over.

The walls sighed. The chamber shivered. And the game moved forward once more.

SEVEN

The cards floated above the table, their edges glowing faintly in the dim torchlight. They hovered, shifting positions watching as invisable hands shuffled them in slow, deliberate motions. The weight of the silence in the room pressed down on them, thick and suffocating. No one moved. No one breathed.

Rachel's fingers twitched at her side. She could feel the pull of the game, a force neither seen nor understood urging her forward. The last time they had drawn, it had nearly killed them. But hesitation meant nothing in this house. It demanded participation.

Janey swallowed hard, her voice barely a whisper. "What happens if we don't play?"

Maria, still catching her breath from their escape, pressed a hand to her temple, trying to calm the throbbing inside her skull. "I don't think that's an option."

The cards stopped shuffling.

A single card flipped itself over in the air and floated gently down to the table.

The Ace of Hearts.

A low hum vibrated through the walls. The torches flickered. The ancient symbols carved into the stone began to glow, pulsing with an eerie rhythm, as though the chamber itself had come alive.

Olivia took an uneasy step forward. "What does that mean?"

No answer came. Instead, the room reacted.

The walls shuddered, stone grinding against stone. Then, impossibly, they *expanded*. The space around them stretched, elongating into an impossible void. The chamber no longer felt enclosed—it felt *endless*. The darkness at the edges of their vision seemed to breathe, shifting like something alive, curling toward them.

And then the whispers started again.

Not from the walls.

From the *cards*.

Rachel clenched her jaw, her mind reeling. The voices weren't distorted this time. They were clear. Familiar.

"Five years ago, you walked away."

Her stomach clenched. The voice was unmistakable.

Jeremy.

The sound of his voice sent an electric jolt through her body. She turned sharply, eyes darting around the ever-expanding chamber. He wasn't here. He *couldn't* be here.

"Rachel." The whisper curled through the air like smoke. "Why did you leave me?"

Her knees nearly buckled.

Maria stepped beside her, watching her carefully. "What is it?"

Rachel shook her head, pressing her palms to her temples. "It's not real. None of this is real."

But the whispers didn't stop.

"You made a promise. You broke it."

She knew the memory well. The night Jeremy had called her, desperate, his voice shaking over the phone. She hadn't answered. She had *chosen* not to answer. And the next day, he was gone.

The air around them grew colder. The torches dimmed, their blue flames flickering, threatening to snuff out entirely.

The others weren't unaffected.

Maria's breath hitched, her hand going rigid at her side. Her own whispers had begun. "Mom?" she murmured, barely audible.

The voice that answered was soft. *Broken*. "You let me die."

Maria stumbled backward, colliding with Olivia, who had gone pale as a sheet. "No," Olivia whispered, shaking her head, her arms wrapping around herself. "No, that's not—"

The air trembled.

The torches *died*.

In the instant of complete darkness, something moved.

Not just the shadows.

Something else.

The cards scattered off the table, flinging themselves into the air like a whirlwind had ripped through the chamber. The whispers rose into a chaotic cacophony of accusations, regrets, lost voices from the past that clawed at them, dragging them backward in time.

Janey screamed. Not in fear—but in *rage*. "Enough!"

The whispers stopped.

The chamber snapped back into reality.

The torches flared back to life, casting flickering light over their stunned faces. The cards settled, drifting gently back onto the table as if nothing had happened.

Maria's breath came fast, uneven. She pressed a shaking hand to her chest. "It's playing with us. It *knows* us."

Caroline's voice was tight. "It's using our past against us."

Rachel exhaled shakily. "We don't give in."

The voice returned, smooth as silk, curling around them like a serpent.

"Then let's raise the stakes."

The table groaned, the cards reshuffling themselves. A new one flipped over on its own.

The Queen of Spades.

A slow, deliberate *knock* came from somewhere in the chamber.

And then, the walls began to *bleed*.

Thick, black ichor oozed from the carvings, slithering down the stone like veins bursting open. The air reeked of decay, of something festering beneath the surface, waiting to be unleashed.

Maria clenched her fists. "We need to get out of here."

Rachel reached for the deck, but before her fingers could touch the cards, the walls *shifted*.

The chamber no longer had doors.

They were sealed inside.

Then, from the black veins in the walls, something *crawled out*.

The figure that emerged was wrong—its limbs too long, its joints bending at unnatural angles. Its face was blank, featureless, yet they *felt* it watching them. It jerked forward in sharp, spasmodic movements, the wet sound of its approach echoing in the sealed chamber.

Olivia let out a choked sob, backing away until her shoulders met the cold stone wall. "No, no, no—"

The creature tilted its head, the sound of bones grinding together filling the silence. A mouth slowly split open across its smooth face, stretching too wide, revealing jagged, gnarled teeth. A voice slithered from its throat, a rasping mimicry of Jeremy's. "Rachel… you left me."

Rachel felt the bile rise in her throat, her hands trembling. "You're not real."

The thing *laughed.*

Janey grabbed Rachel's wrist and yanked her back as the creature *lunged.* Its elongated fingers scraped the stone where Rachel had stood moments before, leaving deep, jagged grooves in the rock.

"MOVE!" Maria shouted.

They scattered, dodging the creature as it twisted unnaturally, its movements eerily smooth despite its grotesque shape. The torches flared, casting frantic shadows that made it seem like there were more of them—more creatures lurking just beyond the edge of sight.

The game wasn't just playing with them anymore.

It was *hunting* them.

Then, as if the walls themselves had been listening, the chamber *lurched.* The stone beneath them cracked like a hollow shell, splitting open to reveal an abyss so deep it swallowed the torchlight whole.

A cold wind rushed up from below, carrying whispers not of regret, but *laughter.* Mocking, twisted laughter that slithered into their ears like a promise.

The creature lunged again, this time faster. Its fingers skimmed Rachel's shoulder, its nails like ice-cold knives. A sharp, burning sensation spread across her skin as she stumbled forward.

Janey grabbed her, dragging her away from the edge of the chasm. "We can't stay here!"

Maria's eyes locked on the floating deck of cards, still untouched on the table. "The game wants us to play."

Rachel turned, her breath ragged. "Then we end it. Now."

But as she reached for the deck, a hand—rotted, skeletal—*shot out from the void beneath them* and wrapped around her wrist.

The chasm widened, the wind howling now, as more hands clawed their way up from the darkness.

EIGHT

Rachel screamed, her body jerking violently as the skeletal hand clenched around her wrist, its grip like ice burning into her skin. The fingers were gnarled, blackened, the bones splintered in places as if they had been broken repeatedly and healed wrong. The stench of rot curled around her, seeping into her lungs like a sickness, making her stomach churn. Her vision swam, her mind teetering between fight and surrender. A voice, not her own, whispered insidiously in her head—*Why fight? It's easier if you just let go...*

"Rachel!" Maria lunged forward, grabbing her other arm, pulling hard, but the grip of the hand only tightened, dragging her closer to the abyss. The chasm below pulsed, shifting like it was alive, filled with *things* that should not exist. Eyes, too many of them, blinked up from the darkness, watching, waiting. The abyss knew their weaknesses. It could smell their fears.

Another hand shot out, this one grasping for Olivia's ankle. She shrieked, kicking wildly, her boot connecting with the brittle bones, shattering them into dust. But as soon as they broke, more emerged, reaching, grasping, desperate. The pit was hungry.

"Get her free!" Janey shouted, her voice raw with desperation. She grabbed the nearest torch from the wall, the blue flame flaring wildly in her grip. Without hesitation, she jammed the burning tip against the skeletal fingers encasing Rachel's wrist. The bones hissed and shrieked, writhing like something alive, then crumbled to ash.

Rachel stumbled backward, gasping, clutching her wrist where the bruises had already begun to bloom. Her heartbeat slammed against her ribs, her mind spinning with intrusive thoughts. *You were almost gone. One second longer, and you would have been free of it all...*

"That's new," she panted, her voice unsteady. "Apparently, they *burn*."

"Then we use that." Maria yanked another torch from the wall, tossing it to Olivia. "If they want to drag us down, we fight back."

But the pit was *changing*.

The stone around it began to crack, webbing outward like shattered glass. The whispers rising from below grew louder, no longer distorted but *distinct*. Voices, layered on top of one another, some begging, some laughing, some chanting in an ancient language that made Rachel's head throb with nausea. She pressed her hands to her temples, trying to silence them, but they only grew louder, creeping into the corners of her consciousness, peeling apart her sense of reality.

Then the game decided to *move forward*.

The deck of cards lifted again, spinning midair, flickering in and out of focus like a bad signal. One by one, they flipped, revealing their fate.

The Jack of Diamonds.

A horrible, guttural *laugh* filled the chamber. The walls pulsed, the torches dimmed, and then the temperature *plummeted*.

The air grew so frigid that their breath crystallized instantly. Frost cracked along the stone walls, spider-webbing outward, creeping toward them. A gust of wind, impossibly cold, slammed into them, nearly knocking them off their feet. It was as if the pit itself had exhaled.

"What the hell is happening?" Olivia shivered violently, wrapping her arms around herself. Her teeth chattered, but it wasn't just the cold. It was the *voices*. They were in her head now too, whispering things she thought she had buried long ago.

The laughter *deepened*.

From the shadows beyond the pit, something *stepped forward*.

At first, it looked human. But as it moved closer, the illusion crumbled.

Its body was elongated, stretched too thin, its limbs moving like marionette strings were pulling them into place. Its face—or what was *left* of it—was frozen in a grotesque grin, lips peeled back to reveal shattered, jagged teeth. Frost clung to its hollow eye sockets, where twin black voids stared out, unblinking. The moment it locked onto them, an unbearable pressure settled onto their chests, like the weight of hands pressing down, suffocating them with terror.

"It's the Jack," Maria whispered, gripping the torch tighter. "The card wasn't just a symbol. It's a rule. A piece of the game."

The Jack tilted its head sharply, bones cracking like breaking ice. Its mouth opened—too wide—and the cold deepened.

Rachel felt it immediately. The cold wasn't just physical. It was inside her, wrapping around her ribs, squeezing her lungs. Her vision blurred. Something whispered at the edges of her thoughts, beckoning her to listen, to *let go*.

Caroline gasped, her hands trembling. "It's *draining* us. It's getting inside our heads."

Janey gritted her teeth. "We're not playing by its rules. We make our own."

She took a step forward, the torch raised high, but the Jack *moved*.

One moment it was across the chamber, the next it was inches from her face.

She barely had time to react before a hand of ice wrapped around her throat.

She choked, the breath stolen from her lungs in an instant. Frost bloomed across her skin, spidering up her neck, her lips turning blue. And then she heard it—her own voice, from years ago, echoing in her head.

You'll never be enough.

You ruin everything you touch.

They'd all be better off if you weren't here.

The words crushed her, the weight of every fear, every insecurity, pressing down like an avalanche. The Jack *knew* her. It knew *all* of them. It was inside their minds, carving out their weakest spots, their ugliest wounds, and turning them against themselves.

"JAN—" Maria lunged, swinging her torch, the flame slicing through the Jack's arm. It *shrieked*, a sound that made every nerve in their bodies *scream*, and recoiled.

Janey collapsed, gasping, her skin raw with cold burns. Tears streamed down her face, not from pain, but from the brutal truth the Jack had forced her to relive.

"No more," Rachel growled. "No more playing defense. We end this."

The deck of cards trembled. Another card flipped.

The King of Clubs.

The chamber *shook*. The game wasn't *done* with them yet.

Then, a sound echoed beyond the walls—a door creaking open, heavy footsteps approaching.

Someone was coming.

Rachel's breath hitched. "No one else is in this house but us."

"That's where you're wrong," a voice said, low, raspy, weathered by years of secrets.

They turned sharply, and there, standing in the doorway, was a man—grizzled, his face worn with time and knowledge. His eyes held something they hadn't seen in themselves since the game started.

Recognition.

"You don't beat the game," he said, stepping forward. "You survive it. And I should know… I've played before."

The house groaned, as if in warning.

The game had just changed.

His voice was urgent. "If you want to live, follow me. You have *seconds* before it realizes I'm here."

Janey, still gasping for breath, whispered, "Who... who are you?"

The man's eyes darkened. "The only one who made it out before. But it never let me go." He looked over his shoulder, a shudder rippling through him. "And now, it knows I'm back."

Then the walls *shifted*—closing in around them, swallowing the room behind them whole. The game was not done. It was only *beginning*.

NINE

The walls groaned, twisting and pulsating as if the house itself was alive, responding to their every breath. Dust rained down from the ceiling, coating their hair and clothes like remnants of something ancient crumbling around them. The stranger didn't hesitate—he turned on his heel and bolted down the hallway, his heavy boots echoing against the floorboards.

"Move!" he barked. "You hesitate, you die!"

Rachel's legs obeyed before her mind could catch up, her adrenaline overriding every other instinct. The others followed, their panicked breaths mixing with the guttural moans of the house resisting their escape. The air thickened, the scent of old wood and something *rotting* clogging their throats as they ran.

"Who the hell are you?" Olivia panted, her voice barely carrying over the chaos.

"Not the time!" the man snapped, gripping a rusted doorknob at the end of the hallway. He twisted it violently, but the door refused to budge. A long, rattling exhale slithered through the air, the temperature dropping so fast their breath came out in white puffs. The Jack of Diamonds was near.

The door *shrieked* open at the last second. The man shoved Maria inside first, then yanked Janey in with one rough pull. Rachel stumbled through next, gasping as she crashed against an old wooden table, sending a stack of dusty books flying. Olivia was right behind her, hands shaking as she slammed the door shut.

A beat of silence.

Then—a deafening *bang* against the door.

The wood splintered inward, but the stranger threw his full weight against it, barring it shut. His breath came fast, shoulders heaving as he listened. A slow, deliberate *scraping* sound echoed from the other side, like nails dragging down the surface. The girls held their breath, their bodies stiff with terror.

"It knows we're here," he murmured.

Rachel's pulse hammered in her ears. "What *is* that thing?" she whispered, her voice shaking.

The stranger didn't answer right away. He turned toward the room, his sharp eyes scanning their surroundings. It looked like an old study, filled with towering shelves of books and dust-covered furniture. Cobwebs stretched across the corners, undisturbed for what looked like *decades*.

"This used to be a safe room," he muttered under his breath, running a hand along one of the bookshelves as if searching for something. "If we're lucky, it still is."

"Lucky?" Janey snapped, hugging herself. "You dragged us into another damn room in this *house*! How is that lucky?!"

He turned to her then, his expression unreadable. "Because if we had stayed out there, we'd be dead."

Silence settled over them, thick and suffocating.

"Start talking," Maria demanded, stepping closer. "Who are you? How do you know about the game?"

The man exhaled through his nose, like he'd been dreading this conversation. "Name's Detective Elias Kennedy, local police," he said finally, his voice rough with age and exhaustion. "I grew up in this town, and I became a detective to understand the horrors that took place here. This house... this *game*—it's been here longer than any of us. I played it once. Years ago. And I survived."

Rachel swallowed hard. "How?"

Elias's gaze darkened. "I ran."

Maria frowned. "That's it? You just *left*?"

Elias's jaw clenched. "Not exactly." His fingers traced along the spines of the books, then paused. Slowly, he pulled one from the shelf—an old leather-bound tome, the cover cracked with age. "This game doesn't let people leave. Not really. It follows. It *infects*. And if you make it out, it doesn't forget."

Olivia shuddered. "So why come back? Aren't the police involved?"

Elias hesitated, then flipped the book open. The pages were filled with symbols, old and unfamiliar. "Because it called me. And because the things that lurk in this house... they don't stay inside it. If this game isn't stopped, it will spread. It *wants* to spread. And because if I don't end this, no one else will."

Rachel stepped closer, her eyes scanning the pages. "What is this?"

"The house's history," Elias muttered. "And maybe, if we're lucky, a way to stop the game before it kills us all."

A cold *knock* rattled the door behind them. The lights flickered.

Then, from the darkness outside, a voice whispered.

"Elias... you came back."

His blood ran cold.

"Oh, hell." He snapped the book shut and looked at the girls. "Run. Now."

They bolted for the other side of the room, where an arched doorway led into a winding corridor. The walls trembled, dust cascading from the ceiling as the voice in the darkness deepened into a low, guttural growl. Shadows slithered along the floor, stretching toward them like ink spilled over the wood.

"Faster!" Elias barked, pushing past them.

Rachel barely had time to register the *thing* lunging through the study door. It wasn't just the Jack of Diamonds anymore—this was something worse. A towering figure, its body a mass of writhing limbs, its face indistinguishable, blurred, constantly shifting into different expressions—rage, agony, hunger. It screeched, the sound scraping against her skull like metal on bone.

Elias yanked open a hidden panel along the corridor wall. "Down here!"

Maria was the first to slip through, then Olivia and Janey. Rachel hesitated, watching the creature *melt* through the study entrance, its form seeping into the cracks of the wood, reforming on the other side like liquid darkness. Its hollow sockets fixated on her.

"Rachel!" Elias snarled, grabbing her wrist and pulling her down just as the creature lunged.

They tumbled into a narrow passageway, Elias slamming the panel shut just in time. The walls around them trembled violently as something *massive* slammed against it from the other side.

"It won't hold for long," Elias muttered, pulling them deeper into the passage. "We need to get out of here. Now."

Rachel gasped for air, clutching the wall for support. "How?"

Elias turned to her, his face grim. "There's a way out through the basement. If we're lucky, it hasn't changed since last time."

Maria clenched her fists. "And if it has?"

He hesitated, his silence heavy with meaning.

"Then we hope we're faster than it is."

A bloodcurdling *howl* filled the passage, shaking the very foundation of the house.

They ran.

But something else stirred beneath the floors, deep in the bowels of the house. The wood beneath their feet *groaned*, warping as if something on the other side was pushing against it.

Elias suddenly stopped, his eyes locked onto the darkness ahead. "We're not alone down here."

A new sound emerged from the basement below. A slow, wet *dragging* noise, like something heavy being pulled across stone.

Rachel's fingers dug into the damp walls. "What now?"

Elias exhaled sharply. "Now we pray we're not too late."

From somewhere in the shadows, a *voice* whispered—a childlike giggle, distant yet *close*.

The house had been expecting him.

TEN

Elias's fingers danced over the spines of the bookshelves, searching. "There should be a passage here," he muttered under his breath, frustration etching his voice. "It was here before."

"The house changes, remember?" Rachel said, gripping a nearby chair as another violent shudder ran through the walls. The whispers beyond the door were growing *stronger*, more insistent.

A distant *click* sounded as Elias's fingers pressed against a loose brick. The bookshelf shuddered and groaned before shifting open, revealing a pitch-black tunnel.

"Go!" he ordered, shoving Maria forward.

One by one, they stumbled into the hidden passage, the air thick with dust and mildew. The moment Elias stepped in behind them, the bookshelf slammed shut.

The tunnel walls were damp, pulsing as if the house itself *breathed*. Shadows slithered across the ceiling, curling toward them with claw-like tendrils.

"We keep moving," Elias instructed, his voice taut. "Don't stop, don't turn around, and don't listen to anything you hear."

Rachel swallowed, gripping Maria's sleeve. "Listen to *what*?"

As if in response, a sound rose behind them—a distorted chorus of voices. *Help me... please...* The words slithered through the air, soft at first, then growing louder. *Don't leave us down here...*

Janey let out a strangled cry. "Those voices..."

"They're not real," Elias snapped. "The house is *testing* us. It knows we're close."

A burst of icy wind rushed through the tunnel, extinguishing their light. For a single, agonizing moment, they were *blind*.

Then—

A distant glow ahead.

"The exit!" Olivia gasped, breaking into a run.

They burst through a rusted metal door, stumbling out into the night. The freezing air hit them like a wall as they staggered out onto the street, lungs heaving. The moment Elias slammed the door shut, the entire house *shuddered*. The windows flickered with an eerie blue glow before going dark. The silence that followed was unnatural—like the house was *watching*, waiting.

"We made it..." Janey gasped, hands on her knees. "Oh my god, we actually made it out."

Rachel turned toward Elias, her voice raw. "That thing inside—it knew your name. It *knew* you."

Elias's expression was grim. "It remembers everyone who's ever played."

Maria took a deep breath, still shaking. "Now what?"

Elias glanced down the empty street, then motioned for them to follow. "Come with me. There's a place we can talk."

They walked for several blocks in silence, the oppressive weight of the night lingering over them. Every shadow felt *too deep*, every alleyway stretched longer than it should have. The town itself seemed quieter than it should be.

Eventually, Elias led them to a small, dimly lit coffee shop tucked between a row of closed storefronts. The neon sign above flickered: *Midnight Brews*.

Inside, the air smelled of burnt coffee and old wood. A tired-looking waitress glanced up from behind the counter, barely acknowledging them before returning to her crossword puzzle. Elias led them to a booth in the back, away from the windows.

Once they were seated, he leaned forward, resting his forearms on the table. His eyes were dark with something unreadable. "You want the truth? Fine. But once I tell you, there's no going back."

Rachel exhaled shakily. "We were *never* going back after tonight."

Elias nodded slowly. "The game..." he hesitated, then ran a hand through his hair. "It doesn't just *trap* people. It takes them. It changes them. And sometimes... if it doesn't get what it wants, it *sends them back*—wrong."

The table was silent.

"I played when I was seventeen," he continued. "And I lost people. My friends. The game swallowed them, and I was the only one who made it out. Or at least, that's what I thought. Until they started showing up again. In my dreams. In shadows on the street. Sometimes, I'd hear them whisper my name—just like tonight."

Rachel shivered. "You think they're still in there?"

Elias exhaled. "I *know* they are. And if we don't stop this, none of us are going to be the same when it's over."

The lights in the café flickered.

Somewhere outside, the wind howled.

And in the reflection of the window, just for a moment, something else stared back at them.

ELEVEN

Elias sat in his police cruiser just outside the precinct, gripping the steering wheel tighter than he realized. His mind reeled from the night's events—the way the house *shifted*, how the game *adapted*, and worst of all, how it had spoken his name like an old friend. He exhaled sharply and ran a hand down his face before stepping out of the car.

Inside, the station was nearly empty, the late hour leaving only a skeleton crew. The air smelled of stale coffee and paperwork, the low hum of fluorescent lights filling the silence. Officer Grant sat behind the dispatch desk, barely looking up from his screen.

"Rough night, Kennedy?" Grant muttered, sipping from his chipped coffee mug.

Elias nodded but didn't elaborate. He wasn't in the mood to explain why he smelled like mildew and fear.

"Got a couple of calls about weird noises from the old MacArthur place," Grant added. "Dispatch figured it was kids messing around again, but I put it in the log." He paused, giving Elias a side glance. "You were out there, weren't you?"

Elias sighed. "Yeah."

Grant shook his head. "You know better."

"I know," Elias muttered. "I had no choice."

Without another word, he made his way to his office, shutting the door behind him. The room was small, lined with case files and newspaper clippings pinned to the walls. Headlines screamed back at him:

MISSING TEENS LAST SEEN NEAR OLD MACARTHUR HOUSE.

LOCAL FAMILY DISAPPEARS—HOME ABANDONED.

ANOTHER VICTIM OF THE GAME? TOWN LEGENDS PERSIST.

Elias ran a hand through his hair and collapsed into his chair, his exhaustion threatening to consume him. But there was no time for rest. If the game was active again, then they were already running out of time.

He pulled open a rusted filing cabinet and began flipping through old reports. Some were decades old, yellowed with age, the ink fading. His fingers hesitated over one particular file, a name he hadn't seen in years—*Nathaniel Carter, missing at seventeen. Last seen entering the MacArthur House with three friends. None were ever found.*

His throat tightened. He had known Nathaniel. They had played football together in high school. Nathaniel had been the first to disappear, but not the last.

He kept going, scanning reports from every decade. The pattern was unmistakable—groups of kids daring each other to enter the house, none of them ever coming back. Each report detailed the same thing: *No signs of forced entry. No signs of struggle. As if they had simply… vanished.*

Elias pulled another report, this one from 1979. Four teenagers, gone without a trace. The only clue? A deck of cards left behind at the threshold, the top card flipped face up: *The Queen of Spades*.

A flicker of movement caught his eye in the corner of the office.

He froze.

His breath came out shallow as he turned his head slowly, but nothing was there. Just the dim light from the desk lamp casting shadows against the wall. But for a moment, he *swore* he had seen something standing there.

Shaking it off, he continued flipping through the reports. But as his fingers traced the old documents, a cold chill pressed against the back of his neck.

Then, a whisper.

Low. Garbled. Right in his ear.

You left us, Elias.

His entire body went rigid. His pulse roared in his ears. The room was *empty*—he knew that. He had locked the door.

Slowly, he turned his head, dreading what he might see. But there was nothing. Only his office, quiet except for the hum of the overhead light.

His eyes drifted back to the files, but his breath caught in his throat.

The report in front of him was open to a picture of Nathaniel Carter. But Nathaniel's face… it had changed.

His once youthful smile had twisted into something unnatural—his eyes sunken, mouth stretched too wide in a grotesque grin.

Elias shoved back from his desk, his chair scraping loudly against the floor. The moment he blinked, the picture was normal again.

A hallucination.

It had to be.

His hands trembled as he reached for his coffee, desperate for something *real* to ground himself. He was exhausted. That was all. His mind was playing tricks on him.

But deep down, he knew better.

The game wasn't just spreading.

It was *inside* him now.

A knock at the door jolted him.

Before he could react, the door creaked open slightly, and a familiar voice called out, "Elias?"

Detective Paul Mercer stepped inside, his expression shifting from neutral curiosity to immediate concern. "Jesus, you look like hell. What's going on?"

Elias exhaled shakily, rubbing his temples. "I was at the MacArthur House."

Mercer's face darkened instantly. "You *what*? Elias, tell me you're screwing with me."

Elias let out a humorless chuckle. "Wish I was."

Mercer shut the door fully, lowering his voice. "Why the hell would you go back there? We don't go *near* that place."

Elias sighed, rubbing a hand over his face. "Because it's happening again. The game's awake. And this time, it's not just targeting kids breaking in for fun. It's *expanding*—pulling in new people. People who have nothing to do with it."

Mercer swallowed hard, taking a slow step closer. "You sure?"

Elias gestured toward the stack of reports on his desk. "Look at these cases, Paul. They're all the same. The disappearances, the patterns. It's all connected. And tonight, I watched that damn house move—*breathe*—like it was *alive*."

Mercer stiffened, his jaw working as he processed the words. He took a slow breath, then muttered, "Dammit."

Elias leaned back, exhaustion sinking into his bones. "You believe me?"

Mercer let out a dry laugh. "Of course I believe you. You think I don't know what that place is? We don't talk about it for a *reason*, Elias. You remember Officer Martinez? The one who wouldn't even drive past that street after 2004? He wasn't crazy. He saw something. *We all have.* But we pretend we don't. It's easier that way."

Elias shook his head. "I can't pretend, Paul. Not when people are dying."

Mercer looked down at the files, then back at Elias. "So what do we do?"

Elias exhaled. "We start with them. The girls who made it out tonight. They're already part of it. They need to know everything."

Mercer ran a hand through his hair. "Then you better pray we're not already too late."

Twelve

Janey double-checked the locks for the third time that night, her hands trembling as she slid the deadbolt into place. The faint hum of the central heating was the only sound in the house, save for the occasional creak of the old wood settling. Every noise set her nerves on edge.

Maria sat on the couch, staring blankly at her phone. "No signal," she muttered. "Figures."

Olivia hugged her knees to her chest in the armchair, her face pale and drawn. "Even if we could call someone, what would we say? 'Hey, a haunted house tried to kill us. Think you could send someone over?'" She laughed dryly, but there was no humor in it.

Rachel sat cross-legged on the floor, pressing her palms to her temples. "We need a plan. We can't just sit here and pretend that didn't happen."

Janey turned from the door, exhaling shakily. "We need to figure out what this *thing* wants. Elias said the game doesn't just end. It *follows*. That means it's not over just because we're out of that house."

"Then what do we do?" Olivia asked, looking up. "Wait for it to come knocking? Because I'm not opening that door again."

Maria finally set her phone down and rubbed her temples. "We listen to Elias. We need to hear what he knows before we make any decisions."

Rachel's expression darkened. "That's assuming we make it to morning."

A deep silence settled over them. No one spoke for a long time.

Then—

A soft *tap* at the window.

Olivia sucked in a sharp breath, her fingers digging into the armrest of the chair. "Tell me someone *did not* just hear that."

Maria slowly turned her head toward the front window. The curtains were drawn tight, blocking any view of the outside. But the soft, rhythmic tapping continued.

Rachel got to her feet, her entire body rigid. "No one move."

Janey swallowed, her voice barely above a whisper. "It's testing us."

The tapping stopped.

For a long moment, there was only silence.

Then, a voice.

Muffled. Familiar.

"Let me in."

Janey's blood ran cold.

Rachel clenched her fists. "That's... that's not possible."

Maria's voice was barely audible. "That sounded like *Elias*."

But they all knew better. Elias was at the precinct. He wouldn't be standing outside in the freezing dark, whispering through the window.

Rachel shook her head. "Don't answer it. Don't even go near it."

The house *creaked*, as if reacting to their fear. The voice at the window spoke again, more insistent this time. "Janey. Maria. Rachel. Olivia. Let me in."

It *knew their names*.

Maria grabbed Janey's wrist. "We need to get away from the windows."

They backed toward the hallway, their breaths shallow, their minds racing.

Then the air *changed*—a pressure so thick it made their ears pop. A shadow slithered beneath the front door, stretching unnaturally across the wooden floor. The temperature dropped, breath misting in the air as a slow, deliberate *scratching* sound began at the base of the door, dragging up toward the handle.

Janey choked on a breath. "It's *inside*."

Olivia let out a whimper, pressing herself against the wall. "No. No, no, no, we locked everything. It can't—"

A whisper, directly in Rachel's ear.

"You think locks will keep me out?"

Rachel *screamed*, stumbling backward into Maria, knocking them both to the floor. The house *groaned*, as if *laughing* at them.

Shadows twisted along the walls, stretching into grotesque, elongated figures, their limbs bending at impossible angles. The air pulsed with an unnatural energy, like the moment before a lightning strike. A low, guttural *chuckle* reverberated through the room, vibrating deep in their chests.

Then, the whispering returned, but this time it wasn't just one voice.

They're waiting for you.
You never left.
The game isn't over.

The tapping resumed, harder this time, turning into *pounding*.

Janey clenched her teeth and squeezed her eyes shut. "We have to hold out until morning. We have to—"

A loud *BANG* rattled the entire house, making the walls tremble. The lights flickered violently, casting jagged shadows that twisted and writhed as if alive.

Maria grabbed Rachel's arm, yanking her to her feet. "We can't just sit here!"

Rachel's breathing was ragged. "Then what? If we run, where do we go?"

Olivia pointed to the hallway. "Janey's dad's old gun—he kept it in the closet, right?"

Janey nodded, her body trembling. "Yes, but—"

Another *bang*, this time from the back door.

They weren't alone.

Janey sucked in a shaky breath. "We move together. No one separates."

Rachel nodded, wiping the sweat from her forehead. "Right. And if that thing gets in—"

Maria's jaw tightened. "Then we fight."

The pounding on the walls escalated, echoing through the house like a heartbeat.

And through it all, a single, drawn-out whisper seeped through the cracks in the doorframe.

"You're still playing."

Then, suddenly, the sound *stopped*. The house fell into an eerie silence, as if the entity had retreated—or worse, had found a new way inside.

Rachel exhaled shakily. "Why did it stop?"

Maria shook her head. "Maybe it's waiting."

Janey's eyes darted to the shadows stretching across the ceiling, twisting unnaturally even though no light moved. "Or maybe it already *got in* some other way."

A sickening *creak* came from the basement door.

They all turned toward the sound at once. The door was shut, but the knob twitched—slowly, methodically—like something was testing it from the other side.

Then, a small, childish giggle echoed from behind the door.

Rachel's breath hitched. "No..." she whispered. "No, no, no—"

A single word scratched against the wood like fingernails:

"Ready?"

THIRTEEN

Elias stood outside an unassuming brick building on the outskirts of town, his breath curling in the cold night air. The wooden sign hanging above the door read *The Hollow Veil Apothecary*, but the locals who knew better called it something else—*The Circle's Keep*.

He hesitated for only a moment before pushing open the door. A small brass bell jingled, announcing his arrival. Inside, the air was thick with the scent of burning sage, dried lavender, and something far more ancient, something that sent a prickle down his spine. Shelves lined the walls, filled with jars of herbs, bundles of dried roots, and candles of every shape and color. This wasn't just a shop. It was a sanctuary, a place where the forces of the world could be felt humming beneath the surface.

A woman emerged from behind the counter, her presence commanding but calm. She was tall, with dark, intelligent eyes that seemed to see straight through him. Her silver-threaded hair was braided back, and her voice, when she spoke, was firm and knowing.

"Detective Kennedy," she greeted. "We were expecting you."

Elias stiffened. "Of course you were."

From the back of the shop, two more figures stepped into the candlelight. One was a younger woman with sharp cheekbones and piercing green eyes, the other an older man with a long, weathered face. The three of them radiated a quiet power—one that had been honed over years, maybe centuries. They were more than witches. They were keepers of forgotten knowledge, protectors of the boundary between this world and the next.

"You've come about the game," the woman continued, moving toward a worn wooden table in the center of the room. "You need answers. And we need to know just how bad this has become."

Elias exhaled. "Bad doesn't cover it."

The younger woman, Lillian, crossed her arms. "You saw it move, didn't you? The house. The shadows. The way it *knows*?"

Elias nodded. "And it's not staying contained anymore. It's following them. It's following *me*."

The older man, Elias had met before—Silas Doran, the eldest of the coven, the historian of their craft. He pulled out a thick, aged book, its leather cover stained with time. "Then it's as we feared," he murmured, flipping through brittle pages. "The house has bound itself to the game, and the game has bound itself to *them*."

Elias ran a hand down his face. "So how do we break it?"

The leader of the coven, Miriam Vale, sat across from him and folded her hands. "First, we must understand why it hasn't been stopped before. This game has played itself for *centuries*. Every few decades, new players stumble upon it, thinking it's a joke, thinking it's just an urban legend. But the game has *always* had rules. Those rules have been altered, rewritten, strengthened. And now, it's no longer bound to the house—it has *anchored itself* to the souls who played it."

Silas cleared his throat and placed the old tome in front of Elias. He opened it carefully, revealing faded ink and diagrams drawn in trembling hands. "This game," he said, "did not start as a game at all. It was once a summoning ritual, a contract written in blood by those who sought knowledge forbidden to mortals."

Elias frowned. "A ritual?"

Miriam nodded. "In the late 1600s, a group of men—alchemists, occultists—believed they could cheat death, that they could use the power of the *other side* to grant themselves immortality. They devised a ritual disguised as a game, a deck of cards infused with incantations, each suit representing a different force of nature: hearts for life, spades for death, diamonds for fortune, and clubs for sacrifice."

Lillian's green eyes darkened. "But they didn't account for what they were summoning. The entity that came through… it did not grant them immortality. It *took* them. Their bodies were never found, but the cards remained."

Silas traced a skeletal hand over a page in the book. "The cards became vessels, a doorway for the entity to move through, and over time, the game reshaped itself. What was once a tool for power became something far worse—a curse that latched onto anyone who dared to play. The house, the one you saw moving, was *built around it*—a cage to contain the growing hunger of the entity. But as you have seen, the cage is no longer enough."

Elias clenched his jaw. "And now we've made it stronger."

Miriam's expression was grim. "You have fed it. Every new player, every lost soul—it absorbs them, reshapes itself. The game is no longer just about winning or losing. It's about *feeding* something that should never have been awakened."

Elias swallowed hard. "The girls."

Miriam nodded. "Yes. And you."

Silence stretched between them. The weight of those words settled deep in Elias's chest. He had suspected it since he left the house—that the game wasn't letting him go either. That it never had.

"Then tell me what I have to do," Elias said, his voice steady. "Tell me how we end it."

Lillian stepped forward, laying a spread of old tarot cards onto the table, the edges frayed with use. She turned one over—a card marked with a *hanged man* suspended between life and death.

"This game doesn't want to end," she murmured. "But every game has a final round. If you want to finish it, you have to *play it through*."

Elias's stomach clenched. "You mean—"

Miriam nodded gravely. "Yes. You and the girls must return to where it started. You must *finish* the game. Only then can the house be severed from this plane. Only then can you break its hold."

Elias clenched his jaw. "And if we lose?"

Silas finally looked up from his book, his voice low, edged with something ancient. "Then you don't come back. None of you do."

The candlelight flickered. Outside, the wind howled against the shop's windows, as if something had heard them.

The game was waiting.

Fourteen

The living room felt smaller than before, its walls seeming to close in as Elias spoke. The morning light barely cut through the heavy tension weighing down on everyone. Janey, Maria, Olivia, and Rachel sat on the couch, silent, eyes fixed on Elias as he paced in front of them. The weight of the witches' warnings lingered in the air like smoke, suffocating and inescapable.

"So, let me get this straight," Maria finally broke the silence, rubbing her temples. "We played a game, but it was never a game. It was some ancient ritual, and now we're... what? Bound to it?"

Elias stopped pacing and exhaled sharply. "Yes. The witches confirmed it. The second you drew your first card, you became a part of something that has been feeding for centuries. You weren't just playing. You were offering yourselves up to something that was waiting. Something that has *always* been waiting."

Rachel leaned forward, her arms resting on her knees. "And you? Why is it after you?"

Elias hesitated before answering, the weight of truth pressing on him. "Because I played too. A long time ago. And I never finished."

Silence stretched between them, the implication settling in.

Olivia let out a sharp, bitter laugh. "Great. So you left the game unfinished, and now it's back for *all* of us?"

Elias met her gaze. "I thought I had escaped. I thought if I ran, if I never spoke of it again, it would forget me. But it doesn't forget. It waits. It finds new players. And now, it's stronger than it's ever been. It's tied itself to *us*. The witches believe it has evolved beyond just the house—it has learned how to *attach itself* to people. The spirits inside… they aren't just lost souls. They are *part* of it now. And they want us there with them."

Janey swallowed hard. "And the witches? They think they can stop it?"

Elias nodded. "They're preparing spells, protections, anything that can give us an advantage. But they made one thing very clear—magic alone won't be enough. The game has rules, and the only way to end it is to *finish playing*. And that means confronting the ones who were taken before."

Maria shook her head. "And if we lose?"

Elias didn't answer. He didn't have to.

Rachel inhaled deeply, steeling herself. "Then we don't lose."

As the weight of their situation settled over them, Janey pulled a blanket tighter around her shoulders. "Alright, so what do we do next?"

Elias pulled a folded piece of paper from his pocket and smoothed it out on the coffee table. It was an old hand-drawn map, the paper yellowed and frayed.

"This is the layout of the house," Elias explained. "At least, what it *used to be*. The house shifts—walls move, doors vanish—but the game room, the center of it all, remains the same. That's where we have to go. That's where it *ends*."

Olivia frowned. "How do we even get back inside? The house barely let us *leave*."

Elias glanced toward the window, his jaw tightening. "It will call us back when it's ready. And we have to be ready when it does."

Janey ran a hand through her hair, exhaling sharply. "So, we just... wait for it? That's the plan?"

Elias hesitated. "Not exactly. The witches are preparing a ritual, something that might force the house to reveal its true form, to make it vulnerable. But for that to work, we need to weaken its hold."

Maria crossed her arms. "And how do we do that?"

Elias's expression darkened. "By finding the other players. The ones who never made it out."

Rachel's breath caught in her throat. "You mean—"

Elias nodded grimly. "The ones it *took*. They're still inside. And if we're going to win this, we need to bring them back."

The room fell into stunned silence. The idea of stepping back inside that house was terrifying enough, but searching for those who had already lost?

"You think they're still alive?" Janey asked, her voice barely above a whisper.

"Not in the way you're thinking," Elias admitted. "But if we can find them, if we can sever their connection to the game, we might have a chance."

Maria scoffed. "You mean we might have a chance to become *them*."

Elias didn't argue. He knew the risk. They all did.

He took a deep breath and leaned against the table. "The witches told me something else. The spirits in that house... they aren't just lost. They're *trapped*. Some of them still don't understand that they died playing the game. They don't know time has passed. And they won't trust us. The house warps their memories, bends them to its will. Some will try to stop us. Some will try to *keep us there*."

Janey clenched her fists. "How do we get them back?"

Elias hesitated before answering. "We have to make them remember. We have to show them the truth. And that means going deeper into the game than anyone ever has."

A heavy silence followed his words, the weight of their mission pressing down on them.

The spirits were waiting. The game was waiting. And time was running out.

Fifteen

The walk back to the house felt like a funeral march. The cold morning air did little to shake the growing dread pressing against them. The streets were eerily silent, the town seemingly oblivious to the nightmare unfolding beneath its surface. Shadows stretched unnaturally long across the pavement, as if reaching for them, grasping at the edges of their resolve. The sky had shifted to an unnatural shade of gray, the sun struggling against the creeping mist that curled along the sidewalks like ghostly fingers.

Elias led the way, his posture rigid, every muscle in his body coiled with tension. The girls followed closely, their steps hesitant, as though each movement might summon something lurking just beyond their sight. The eyes bore down on them, and an unsettling awareness settled in their chests—*they were being watched.*

Janey clutched the protective charm one of the witches had given her, the smooth stone warm in her palm despite the morning chill. "I don't feel right about this," she muttered, her voice barely above a whisper.

"You shouldn't," Elias replied without looking back. "The house knows we're coming. It's preparing."

Maria swallowed hard. "Preparing for what?"

Elias slowed his pace, his eyes locked on the horizon where the MacArthur house loomed like an open wound against the sky. The structure looked *wrong*, shifting in and out of focus like a mirage, its silhouette warping with each second they spent looking at it.

"To play," Elias murmured.

They reached the house just as the last remnants of morning light faded behind thick, unnatural storm clouds. The structure was *taller*, its wooden frame groaning as if stretching, expanding to accommodate the game's new round. The windows were black voids, absent of reflection, absent of life. A distant sound, like nails dragging against wood, echoed from somewhere within.

Rachel gritted her teeth. "It's waiting. It *knows* we're here."

Elias stepped onto the porch first, the wooden planks creaking beneath his weight. The air was thick, suffocating, carrying the distinct scent of damp rot and something *fouler*— something old. He turned to face them. "Remember what I said —no matter what happens, *we do not separate*. The house will try to split us up. It will make us see things that aren't real. It will use our memories against us."

Janey nodded, gripping her charm tighter. "And the spirits? The other players?"

Elias's expression darkened. "They might not know they're dead. Some of them may even think they *won*. We have to remind them of the truth."

Maria inhaled deeply, steadying herself. "And if they fight us?"

Elias hesitated before answering. "Then we fight back."

The moment they stepped inside, the air *changed*. It was colder, thicker—like stepping into a different reality. The walls pulsed, breathing in slow, deliberate movements, the wallpaper shifting beneath with force. The front door slammed shut behind them with a deafening *boom*, sealing them inside.

A wind howled through the house, but there were no open windows. The flickering candle sconces lining the walls lit on their own, casting grotesque shadows that *moved*. The scent of damp earth and something decayed permeated the air, making Olivia gag.

"Oh, God," Olivia whispered. "This feels worse than before."

The hallway was long, impossibly long. Doors stretched on endlessly, more than there should have been. Shadows flickered in the corners of their vision, never quite solid but *always there*. The floorboards beneath their feet felt *softer*, as though the wood was decaying beneath them, waiting to swallow them whole.

Olivia shivered. "This wasn't how it looked before."

"It's different every time," Elias murmured. "The house changes to suit the game."

A whisper slithered through the air. Soft, almost gentle. *Come back... finish your turn...*

Rachel turned sharply, her pulse hammering. "Did you hear that?"

Before anyone could respond, the lights overhead flickered violently. The temperature dropped again. Then—

A door creaked open at the end of the hall.

A figure stepped out.

At first glance, he looked normal—a young man, no older than nineteen, with sunken eyes and a slack expression. His clothing was decades out of place, a letterman jacket from a school that no longer existed. His skin was pale, too pale, his hands twitching at his sides like a marionette waiting for its strings to be pulled. His lips curled unnaturally at the corners, stretching too wide in a grin that didn't reach his hollow eyes.

Elias took a slow step forward. "Nathaniel?"

The figure's head snapped up at the name. His voice came too late after the movement, like a bad recording. "You came back."

Elias swallowed hard. "You remember me?"

Nathaniel's eyes flickered with something unreadable. "We're still playing."

Maria's voice was barely above a whisper. "Oh, hell no."

Nathaniel tilted his head, his smile widening as his fingers twitched erratically. "Your turn."

The house groaned, the floor vibrating beneath their feet. The walls began to *close in*, pressing inward, suffocating. The hallway distorted, stretching impossibly long in one moment before snapping back too close in the next, the air thick with the weight of something undetectable.

Suddenly, the air crackled with energy, and a voice boomed from seemingly everywhere at once. "ENOUGH."

A surge of blinding white light split the darkness, and the shadows recoiled, shrieking as the temperature shifted abruptly. The sound of bells—low, rhythmic, pulsing—echoed through the walls, and then, stepping from the void, the witches emerged.

Miriam led them, her eyes burning with something otherworldly as she lifted her staff and struck it against the floor. The house *screamed*. "No more tricks," she hissed.

Lillian raised her hands, and the air seemed to *bend* around her as if reality itself were folding. "It's time to break your hold."

Nathaniel twitched violently, his smile turning into something *wrong*, his face contorting. "You don't belong here," he hissed.

Silas, standing just behind Miriam, whispered an incantation under his breath. A shimmering circle of symbols formed around the group, a barrier against the creeping darkness. "You have no power over them anymore," he declared.

The house *roared*, shaking its very foundation. The walls trembled, cracks forming in the ceiling. *It knew. It felt* the challenge.

Elias turned to the girls. "Now. We finish this."

The game had just changed.

SIXTEEN

The wind howled through the house like a banshee's cry, the walls creaking and groaning under the weight of centuries of trapped souls. Each moan of the ancient structure sent vibrations through their bones, a constant reminder that they were inside something alive—something that hungered. The Housekeeper's presence lingered in every shadow, watching, waiting, as Elias and the others pressed forward through the twisting corridors.

Each step felt like wading through molasses, the very air thick with malevolent energy that sought to slow their progress. The floorboards beneath their feet had grown soft, almost organic, pulsing with each footfall as though they were walking across the belly of some great beast.

"The witches will be here soon," Elias muttered, his voice barely carrying over the house's endless moaning. His fingers traced the grip of the silver dagger at his belt, a gesture that had become almost compulsive since they'd entered. "We have to find Janey before-"

A sharp crack split the air, and the floor beneath them lurched violently. Rachel stumbled, catching herself against the wall, only to recoil as the wallpaper pulsed beneath her touch like living tissue. Her fingers came away sticky with something dark that writhed against her skin.

"Oh God," she gasped, wiping her hand frantically against her jeans. "This place—it's not just haunted anymore. It's becoming something else."

Maria grabbed Rachel's arm, steadying her as another tremor shook the house. "Before what, Elias?" she demanded, her breath coming in short gasps. "Before this place tears itself apart? Before it finishes whatever it's trying to become?"

The house answered for them. The corridor ahead stretched impossibly long, doors appearing and disappearing along its length like teeth in a monster's maw. From somewhere deep within its bowels, a child's laughter echoed—hollow, wrong, a sound that should never have existed.

"Did you hear that?" Olivia whispered, pressing closer to the group. Her fingers were white-knuckled around the protective charm one of the witches had given her, the stone glowing faintly in the darkness. "It sounded like—"

"Don't," Rachel cut her off. "Don't try to make sense of it. That's what it wants."

Elias's jaw clenched as he studied the ever-shifting hallway before them. "We shouldn't have split up. We never should have let her out of our sight."

"The house wanted us separated," Maria said, her voice tight with anger. "It's been planning this from the start, hasn't it? Every move, every turn—it's all been leading to this."

"Yes," Elias admitted, his expression grim. "The game was never random. The house has been testing us, learning our weaknesses. And now..."

The air grew colder, frost crystallizing along the walls in patterns that looked disturbingly like faces frozen in eternal screams. The shadows deepened, coalescing into shapes that lurched and twisted at the edges of their vision. Something wet dripped from the ceiling, but when they looked up, there was nothing there.

A card fluttered down from above, landing face-up at their feet.

The Queen of Spades.

Maria's breath hitched. "It's still playing with us."

"No," Elias growled, snatching up the card. The moment his fingers touched it, the temperature dropped another ten degrees. "It's showing us where to go. The house wants us to find her—but on its terms."

Rachel hugged herself, trying to stop the trembling that had nothing to do with the cold. "Why? What does it gain by leading us to her?"

Elias's expression darkened. "Because whatever's happening to Janey right now, the house wants us to witness it. It wants an audience."

The house shuddered around them, and a door at the end of the hall swung open with a long, agonized creak. Beyond it lay darkness—not the simple absence of light, but something deeper, something hungry. The void seemed to breathe, drawing the shadows toward it like smoke being inhaled.

"Look at the hinges," Maria whispered, pointing to where the door connected to the wall. The metal had fused with the wood, veins of black spreading out from the joints like infection through flesh.

Olivia took a step back, shaking her head. "We can't go in there. Whatever's through that door—it's not part of our world anymore."

Before anyone could respond, a scream tore through the house—Janey's voice, distant but unmistakable. The windows rattled in their frames, and the very foundation seemed to pulse beneath their feet. The sound was followed by something worse—laughter, deep and satisfied, that seemed to come from the walls themselves.

"She's still fighting," Elias said, his voice tight with determination. He pulled the silver dagger from his belt, its blade gleaming with strange symbols etched into the metal. "Which means we still have time."

Rachel grabbed his arm. "You said it yourself—the house is leading us there. This has to be a trap."

"Of course it's a trap," Elias replied, his eyes fixed on the doorway. "But it's the only chance we have. The witches are coming, but they won't be able to stop this on their own. We have to get to Janey before the house finishes whatever it's trying to do."

Maria pulled her own charm from her pocket—a small leather pouch filled with herbs and bones that Miriam had pressed into her hands before they'd entered. "Then we go together. No matter what's through that door, we don't separate again."

They moved forward as one, each step heavier than the last, as if the house itself was trying to hold them back. The shadows reached for them with ghostly fingers, whispering secrets too terrible to comprehend. The air grew thick with the scent of decay and something older—something that had been waiting centuries for this moment.

As they crossed the threshold, Olivia gasped. The room beyond wasn't a room at all—it was an endless void, stretching in all directions. Fragments of the house floated in the darkness like debris in space: doors that led nowhere, windows that showed impossible scenes, staircases that twisted in on themselves in ways that defied physics.

And in the center of it all, a single point of light.

"Janey," Rachel breathed.

She stood alone in the void, her body rigid, her hands clutching something they couldn't quite see. The Housekeeper circled her like a shark, his form shifting between solid and shadow, his smile too wide for his face.

"Welcome," his voice echoed through the impossible space. "We've been waiting for you."

And as they watched in horror, the house began to show its true face. The walls of reality peeled back like burning paper, revealing something vast and ancient stirring in the spaces between. The entity that had been playing with them all along was finally ready to emerge.

The house had been waiting for this moment.

And now, finally, it was ready to claim its prize.

SEVENTEEN

The house did not like being challenged. The moment the witches unleashed their energy, the very walls convulsed, as though the structure itself had a heartbeat. A deep groan reverberated through the air, rattling the floor beneath their feet. The oppressive darkness slithered along the corners of the ceiling, shifting and coiling like a living thing recoiling. The house was not just a place—it was a predator, and it had just been wounded.

But it wasn't giving up.

The house had fed for centuries, drawing in the unwitting and trapping them in its endless cycle. It knew how to bend reality, how to twist the very fabric of existence to its will. And now, these outsiders, these intruders, dared to challenge it? No. It would not allow itself to be weakened. It would retaliate with all the fury of a thing that should never have existed.

Miriam's staff pulsed with a strange luminescence, her lips moving in whispered incantations too ancient for human ears to understand. The symbols glowing beneath their feet burned hotter, growing brighter, as if searing through the house's false reality. The walls seemed to pull away from them, stretching and distorting, as though trying to retreat from the witches' power.

A scream split the air—high-pitched, unnatural. Not just one scream, but many. It came from above, from below, from behind the walls themselves. The house was screaming.

Rachel clutched Olivia's arm, her nails digging into the fabric of her jacket. Her face was pale, sweat glistening on her forehead despite the frigid temperature of the room. "Tell me that was just the house."

"It's fighting back," Elias growled, shifting his stance, his fingers flexing near the hilt of the silver dagger at his belt. His chest rose and fell rapidly, breath pluming in the frozen air. "It's not going to let this happen easily."

Suddenly, the walls lurched. The wooden planks beneath them snapped and buckled, sending them sprawling in different directions. The protective symbols flickered as the house retaliated, distorting reality around them. Janey let out a yelp as she was pulled off balance, her body yanked toward the gaping darkness spreading across the floor.

A putrid stench filled the air—rotting wood, sulfur, and something rancid, like meat left out too long in the summer heat. The scent clawed into their throats, making Olivia gag as she coughed violently, stumbling backward. "God! It smells like something *died* in here."

"No," Miriam said, her voice grim. "It smells like something is *hungry*."

The floor began to pulse, as if something beneath the wood was breathing, waiting. Something massive shifted beneath them, scraping, writhing. The house was not just resisting—it was changing.

"No!" Maria lunged, grabbing Janey's wrist, her feet skidding against the shifting ground. But something was pulling harder, *gripping* Janey's legs as if the shadows had sprouted claws.

"It wants her!" Olivia screamed, her wide eyes darting between Janey's desperate face and the writhing black tendrils creeping toward them.

Miriam slammed her staff against the floor, sending a burst of white-hot energy spiraling outward. The force ripped through the shadows, momentarily severing the house's grip. Janey fell forward into Maria's arms, gasping as though she had been drowning. Her fingers dug into Maria's shoulders, her chest heaving with ragged breaths.

But the house wasn't done.

A loud bang shattered the air, and the doors lining the endless hallway began to shake violently, their frames splintering. One by one, they swung open, revealing figures standing in the darkness beyond.

At first, they looked human—people of all ages, their eyes blank, their expressions eerily neutral. But as they stepped forward, the illusion *peeled away*. Their skin blistered and cracked, mouths stretching open far wider than they should, revealing jagged, blackened teeth. Their eyes turned to pits of abyss, hollow and devouring.

Rachel let out a strangled sob, pressing a trembling hand over her mouth. "Jesus Christ... they're—"

"The lost players," Elias whispered, his voice hoarse, his eyes darting between the grotesque forms. Sweat lined his brow despite the cold, a tremor running through his fingers.

Lillian swore under her breath, her fingers curling into fists. "They're not real anymore. The house has made them part of the game."

One of them, a woman in a torn 1920s dress, lunged at Rachel with unnatural speed. Rachel barely had time to react before Silas stepped forward, throwing a handful of powder into the air. The particles ignited in a burst of golden fire, creating a barrier between them and the advancing spirits.

The spirits *screamed*. Horrible, soul-rattling shrieks that made the walls vibrate. More of them came, their clawed hands reaching through the fire, their movements desperate, furious.

"They don't want us to end the game!" Janey cried, clutching Maria's arm so tightly her knuckles turned white. "They want us to *stay*!"

"They don't have a choice anymore," Elias said grimly, stepping between the group and the spirits. "But we do."

Then a new voice joined the chaos.

"You think you can take them from me?" The voice slithered through the air, low, hungry, and endless. The very sound of it made their skin crawl.

The house shuddered violently as the temperature plummeted. From the darkness of the farthest doorway, a tall figure emerged.

Unlike the spirits, this one was fully formed—no shifting face, no blurred edges of reality. He looked *human*, at least in shape, but his skin was too smooth, too *flawless*, stretched like wax over the bones beneath. His lips curled into a smile, too wide for his face, revealing perfect rows of teeth, each one serrated like the blade of a saw.

His eyes were pure black. Not empty—devouring.

Miriam stilled. The witches stilled. The very air became thick, suffocating.

Elias exhaled sharply, his fists clenching. "The Housekeeper."

The Housekeeper tilted his head, his smile deepening. "It means you've *already lost*."

The house collapsed inward.

The walls folded, the floors vanished, the space around them broke apart like shattered glass, revealing a yawning abyss below. The screams of the lost players merged into an unbearable, discordant wail.

"Draw!" Elias barked.

One by one, they reached for the cards, their hands trembling as they pulled their fate from the deck.

The Housekeeper grinned.

And the house made its final move.

Eighteen

The house had changed. No longer merely a structure, it was a living, *breathing* thing—a labyrinth of nightmares, an entity that had fed upon fear for centuries. Its walls groaned, twisting as though the wood had grown sinews, stretching and *tearing* itself apart with each moment the game continued. The house wasn't just collapsing. It was being reborn.

The air reeked of decay, thick and pungent, the stench curling in their nostrils like something festering deep within the walls. A putrid heat radiated from the wooden floor, damp with something slick and unidentifiable, pulsing as though the very foundation of the house had become a massive, diseased organ.

The floor beneath them cracked and split, revealing a swirling abyss of endless blackness. Elias felt his stomach lurch as gravity seemed to tilt in every direction at once, dragging them toward the chasm that pulsed beneath their feet like a great, open maw. The sound of shifting wood was replaced by something far more sinister—a wet, guttural breathing, low and hungry, vibrating beneath their feet.

"MOVE!" Miriam bellowed, her voice rippling with supernatural power. She slammed her staff into the ground, and for a brief moment, the world steadied.

But then the screaming began again.

The lost players—dozens of them—were climbing out of the walls, out of the ceilings, out of the floors. Their bodies twisted, their faces frozen in expressions of agony and rage. Some had missing eyes, others had mouths that never ended, stretching impossibly down their throats. Skin peeled, fingers curled into claws. They weren't ghosts. They were prisoners, their souls chained to the house, bound to the rules of the game.

Their voices slithered through the air, whispering *nonsense* that should have been incomprehensible, but somehow made too much sense.

"Cold... it's so cold... it never stops..."

"Play your hand, play your hand, play your hand!"

"We waited, we waited, we waited, and you—you—will stay with us."

Some of them had faces that were painfully familiar—figures from news reports, faces from missing posters that had long since been forgotten. A woman in a tattered hospital gown, her face sallow and sunken, the skin around her lips cracked and peeling, whispering prayers with no god left to hear them. A man in a business suit, his tie stained with something black and dripping, his hands trembling as if they had been broken and reset too many times.

Rachel turned and screamed.

A young boy—no older than twelve—lunged at her, his teeth jagged and blackened, his eyes sunken sockets filled with writhing shadows. He didn't move like a child. He moved like a beast. His arms flailed unnaturally, his body contorting as he shrieked, clawing at the air between them.

"NO!" Elias grabbed Rachel and threw her aside, narrowly avoiding the boy's snapping teeth. The child hit the ground, bones cracking sickeningly, but it didn't stop him. He twisted unnaturally, limbs bending backward as he rose again, his mouth splitting open into a void of endless black.

Rachel's breath hitched in terror, her hands trembling violently. "I— I can't—"

"They're not real!" Lillian yelled, hurling a burning sigil at the spirits. The fire exploded upon impact, illuminating their grotesque forms in stark, flickering light. "The house is making them fight for it!"

Janey stumbled backward, her breath ragged as the figures pressed closer. "Then how do we stop them?!"

"We END the game!" Miriam shouted, swinging her staff in a wide arc. Sparks erupted where the staff met the ground, sending out shockwaves that briefly forced the spirits back, but the house was angry now.

The Housekeeper's laughter rippled through the air, low, guttural, and amused.

"End the game?" he echoed, stepping forward, his body flickering like a candle in the dark. His voice was a whisper, a growl, a thousand voices stacked upon one another. "You don't understand, do you? You were never meant to win."

The walls pulsed, shuddered, breathed.

The temperature plummeted, their breath coming out in sharp, white clouds as frost formed on their skin. Their fingers stung with the sudden cold, their joints locking with an unnatural stiffness as the house wrapped them in its influence.

"You are nothing but pieces on a board. Your fate was written the moment you set foot in my house. The only way to end this is to surrender. To become part of it."

Elias steeled his jaw. "That's not happening."

The Housekeeper's eyes gleamed—black as the void, as bottomless as the abyss that threatened to devour them. "Then let's see how long you last."

The entire house lurched downward, as though plummeting into an abyss. The walls around them peeled away, revealing something far worse than darkness.

They were in the heart of the game now.

The air turned thick, *choking*, as though invisible fingers wrapped around their throats. The very fabric of reality unraveled around them, and the players who had been trapped before them crawled closer.

A grotesque gurgling sound echoed through the space as the figures began to whisper, their voices layered upon each other in a haunting, rhythmic chant.

"Stay. Stay. Stay. Stay."

Elias barely had time to react before something cold and *wet* latched onto his wrist. A hand—skeletal and rotting.

He looked down and felt his stomach drop. It was himself.

A rotting, decayed version of Elias—his own corpse, pulled from the depths of the game. Its jaw hung slack, its eyes nothing but dark pits of infinite void. It grinned.

Its voice was wrong, garbled, as though spoken from underwater. "Your turn."

A deep, unnatural snapping sound echoed through the void as the walls of the house convulsed, twisting in on themselves, folding into impossible shapes. The screams of the lost players turned into wails of torment, the sound of hundreds, thousands of souls crying out in unison.

Something huge shifted above them, a great, writhing shadow, its massive shape just beyond the veil of understanding. It coiled, its tendrils snaking through the air, reaching, grasping.

Rachel clutched Janey's arm, her voice nearly hysterical. "We're going to die here!"

"Not if we play the last hand," Elias growled, tearing his arm free from the grasp of his own corpse. It didn't try to stop him. It just grinned wider.

A great, unholy shriek split the world apart.

The Housekeeper's laughter rose, blending with the shrieking of the house, with the suffering of the trapped players, with the unbearable weight of something ancient waking beneath them.

And the game made its next move.

NINETEEN

The house did not simply collapse. It shifted, rewrote itself, bending time and space until nothing was what it seemed anymore. Walls stretched, doorways vanished, and the world around them fractured like a mirror shattering into endless, jagged pieces.

One moment, they were together. The next, they were not.

A force—invisible, unstoppable—ripped them apart.

Elias barely had time to reach for Rachel before she was yanked backward, her scream muffled as the shadows devoured her. He lunged forward, but something invisible struck him hard in the chest, sending him reeling backward. He watched helplessly as she disappeared into the void, her wide, terrified eyes the last thing he saw before she was swallowed whole.

"Rachel!" he bellowed, but the sound was swallowed by the abyss that now stood between them. She was gone.

Maria twisted, her fingers outstretched, but something slammed into her chest, sending her hurtling into darkness. Her screams bounced off the shifting walls, but she was gone before anyone could react. Olivia clawed at the floor, trying to grip something, anything, but the darkness dragged her down, her voice fading as though she had been sucked into another world entirely.

Janey's panicked gaze locked onto Elias for a fraction of a second before the ground beneath her opened up, a black pit spiraling into nothingness. She shrieked as she fell, her hands reaching out to grab the air. Then, silence.

The air tore apart, and everything turned black.

Elias hit the ground hard.

The impact sent a shockwave through his bones, his breath ripping from his lungs as he landed on something wet—not quite solid, not quite liquid. The stench of rotting wood, blood, and something old—something rancid—filled his nostrils. It clung to him, thick as tar, seeping into his clothes and making his skin crawl.

He pushed himself up, his fingers sinking into the floor. It squished beneath his weight, like walking across flesh. The sensation made his stomach churn, nausea roiling in his gut as he staggered to his feet.

He was alone.

The corridor before him stretched unnaturally far, its walls pulsing as if they were alive, shifting like muscle beneath translucent skin. The candle sconces along the walls flickered, their flames blue, their light casting twisted, elongated shadows that moved in ways they shouldn't. Every step he took was followed by a wet squelch beneath his boots, as though the house itself was inhaling and exhaling beneath him.

A whisper slithered through the air, brushing against his ear like breath on the nape of his neck.

"Keep playing, Elias."

His stomach clenched. "Where are they?"

Silence.

Then, from the darkness ahead, a single card fluttered to the ground.

Elias's pulse pounded in his ears as he stepped forward, his boots sinking slightly into the living floor. He reached down, hesitant, but the moment his fingers brushed the card—

A hand shot from the wall, grabbing his wrist.

It was ice-cold, skeletal fingers digging into his flesh, tightening, squeezing. The skin was stretched too thin over its knuckles, the nails long, cracked, and blackened. A low, rattling breath seeped from the wall, carrying with it the scent of decay.

Elias yanked back, but the grip was iron.

His breath caught as his eyes traced the arm back to its owner.

The face emerging from the wall was his own.

A decayed, rotting version of himself, the lips curled into a wide, mocking grin. The mouth opened, but the voice was not his own.

"You should have left when you had the chance."

***

Maria was running.

The hallways were endless. They twisted, curled back into themselves, leading her in circles. The doors she tried wouldn't open. The wallpaper peeled in strips, revealing a glistening, raw surface beneath, like something had been skinned.

A child's laughter rang out from the darkness. Soft at first. Then closer. Closer.

She turned a corner—

And stopped.

In the dim glow of a flickering chandelier, a row of children stood facing the wall. Their clothes were ragged, some from different time periods, others barely more than tattered rags.

Seven of them.

Their backs were to her, their heads bowed, arms at their sides. Their hair was matted with dried blood. One girl's head twitched violently, as if something was jerking her from the inside.

Maria's breathing became ragged. "Who... who are you?"

The children moved.

All at once.

Their heads snapped toward her, their eyes nothing but gaping black holes, their mouths hanging open too wide, too unnatural. Some of them had no lips at all, their teeth clicking together like chattering dolls.

They spoke in unison, their voices a hollow, eerie whisper:

"Your turn."

***

Rachel was in the dining room.

The long mahogany table stretched farther than it should, candlelight flickering off the silverware arranged neatly on the polished surface. The scent of stale wine and decaying food filled the air.

At first, the room seemed empty—but then she saw them.

Seated at the table were the missing players.

Some of them were rotting, their skin hanging in loose, sagging sheets. Others sat stiffly, their eyes locked forward, unmoving, untouched by time. Their plates were filled with unrecognizable meat, some of it still twitching, veins writhing like worms on the bone.

Rachel felt her breath catch. She knew some of these faces.

She had seen them in newspapers, on missing posters, on the town's wall of the forgotten.

The man at the head of the table—he had been missing for over thirty years.

A girl near the end—a teenage runaway who vanished a decade ago.

A young woman with long, brittle hair, her dead eyes locked onto Rachel.

"Sit," the woman whispered, her voice dry, hollow.

The chairs groaned as the dead shifted, making room.

The chair at the far end of the table pulled itself back.

An invitation.

Rachel turned to run.

But the door had vanished.

***

Janey was in the maze.

She couldn't tell how she had gotten here, but the walls of the hedge were pulsing, breathing. The path ahead stretched endlessly, turning sharply at unnatural angles.

Wind howled above her, carrying voices that were almost familiar. The whispers of her mother's voice, the echo of her own childhood laughter. The ground beneath her felt damp, soft—like standing on graves.

But none of it was real.

Janey reached into her pocket, her fingers curling around the small deck of cards she had taken from the last room. Her next move.

A figure stood at the next turn, waiting.
Tall. Motionless.
She recognized him.
A man she had seen once before—on a news broadcast, a town meeting, a file Elias had shown them.
A man who had played this game before.
The Housekeeper smiled.
"Ready for the next round?"

Twenty

Elias's pulse pounded in his ears, his breath shallow and ragged as he stood frozen in front of his own decayed reflection. The thing that wore his face grinned wider, its cracked lips stretching unnaturally, revealing jagged, yellowed teeth. The fingers around his wrist tightened, ice-cold and unyielding, pressing hard enough that his bones ached beneath the pressure.

"Let go," Elias growled, his voice raw with fear he refused to acknowledge.

The thing that was him laughed—a wet, rasping sound that sent a shudder rippling down Elias's spine. "Why? You don't get to leave, Elias. Not this time. Not ever."

The walls around him groaned, the corridor breathing, the walls shifting closer, constricting like a great throat swallowing him whole. The sconces flickered violently, the blue flames distorting, casting writhing shadows that stretched long fingers across the pulsating walls.

With a violent yank, Elias ripped his wrist free from the thing's grip, stumbling back as pain shot up his arm. The hand on the wall convulsed, its fingers twitching before sinking back into the wood with a sickening squelch. The rotten version of himself lingered for a moment longer, those void-dark eyes locking onto him before melting into the wall, leaving behind a faint whisper that sent an unnatural chill into the air.

"Your turn is coming."

Elias turned and ran, his boots slamming against the fleshy floor, the walls pressing inward as he sprinted blindly through the ever-shifting corridors. He called out, his voice hoarse. "Maria! Rachel! Janey! Olivia! Where are you?!" But the house absorbed his words, swallowing them into the shadows.

Maria's heart slammed against her ribs as the children tilted their heads in perfect unison, their gaping mouths stretching into twisted, unnatural grins. The air between them felt thick, almost charged, humming with something powerful.

Her feet refused to move. She tried to scream, but her throat tightened, as though invisible hands had wrapped around her neck. The tallest child—a boy, his face obscured by shadow—took a single step forward. His joints cracked loudly, as though they hadn't moved in decades.

"Maria…"

Her breath caught in her throat.

The boy's voice was her brother's voice.

Her stomach turned to ice. No. No, it wasn't possible. He was dead. He had been dead for years.

Her vision blurred with the sting of tears as the figure stepped fully into the light. The face was wrong, too thin, too sunken, the skin ashen and peeling, but the eyes—the eyes—were his. Wide, desperate, filled with something far worse than recognition.

"You left me," the boy whispered, his cracked lips barely moving. "Why did you leave me?"

Maria shook her head violently. "You're not real."

The boy's mouth twitched, his expression shifting into something unreadable. The children behind him began to hum, a low, droning sound that sent shivers crawling beneath Maria's skin.

The boy raised one shaking hand, palm up, fingers curled. A card appeared between his thumb and forefinger, yellowed and brittle with age.

"Your turn."

Maria let out a strangled sob, stepping backward, her whole body trembling. The walls seemed to close in, the air thick with rot. The children's whispers layered on top of each other, deafening. She screamed.

Rachel pressed herself against the long dining table, her chest rising and falling in short, panicked breaths. The missing players around her sat motionless, their lifeless eyes fixed on her. The chair at the end of the table remained empty, waiting.

She turned, desperate to escape, but her limbs felt leaden, her body betraying her as if she were being held in place by invisible strings.

The man at the head of the table, the one who had been missing for thirty years, lifted his trembling hand. His fingers twitched violently, as if fighting against resistance, before curling around the stem of his wine glass.

Rachel watched, horrified, as he lifted it toward his lips.

Only to pour the thick, black liquid inside down his chest, staining his decayed suit in inky rivulets.

The room shuddered.

The others followed.

One by one, the missing players lifted their glasses, tilting them forward, spilling that same putrid blackness across the pristine white tablecloth. The liquid did not pool—it moved, tendrils of darkness slithering toward Rachel like living things.

A hand brushed her shoulder.

Rachel choked on a scream, spinning to find the woman with brittle hair standing beside her, her cold, dead eyes locking onto her own.

"You should sit," the woman said, voice barely above a whisper.

Rachel tried to move, to pull away, but her body refused. A strangled cry escaped her lips as her legs bent against her will, her knees giving way as she was forced into the empty chair.

The shadows beneath the table shifted.

The house was forcing her to play.

***

Janey's breath came in rapid, shallow gasps as she stood in the endless, pulsing maze. The hedge walls shifted, their veins throbbing beneath a thin layer of something that was not bark.

Wind howled above, but the sound carried whispers that were almost human—soft, pleading, desperate.

Her fingers trembled as she clutched the cards in her hand, their edges sharp enough to cut into her skin. She did not know how long she had been here. Time was slipping. The ground beneath her felt damp, soft—like standing on graves.

A figure stepped forward.

The Housekeeper.

Tall, composed, his presence crushing. His dark eyes gleamed with something unreadable as he lifted his hand, revealing a deck of his own.

"Shall we continue?" he asked smoothly, shuffling the cards between long, pale fingers. "Or do you forfeit?"

Janey's stomach twisted. The Housekeeper had not lost. He had never lost. He was the game.

She heard the others—distant, screaming. Maria's voice, shrill with panic. Rachel sobbing. Elias cursing, his voice raw and desperate.

She could not call back. She could not reach them.

The path behind her vanished.

There was no choice.

Her hands shook as she drew the next card.

The Housekeeper smiled.

And the game went on.

Twenty-One

Elias ran blindly through the suffocating corridors, his breath ragged, his heart hammering against his ribs like a caged animal. The walls shifted around him, stretching and contracting, the wooden panels morphing into something that pulsed like living tissue. Every turn led him deeper into a maze that seemed to be rewriting itself as he moved. He was trapped.

The shadows stretched and slithered along the walls, whispering his name, taunting him in voices that were both his own and those of the long-dead. Mocking. Laughing.

"Elias," a familiar voice rasped from behind him.

He froze, his stomach lurching violently. The air thickened, a deep, rotting scent filling his nostrils. Slowly, hesitantly, he turned.

The thing that wore his father's face stood at the end of the corridor, its head lolling unnaturally to one side. Its flesh sagged, rotted, the sockets of its eyes hollow pits of blackness. A puppet with its strings cut.

Elias's body locked in place, his mind screaming at him to move, to run, but his feet felt rooted to the pulsing, shifting ground.

"You let me die," the figure croaked, stepping forward, its gait jerky, unnatural. "You were supposed to save me, Elias."

His throat tightened. A wave of nausea crashed through him, his legs trembling beneath his weight. He wanted to scream, to call out for the others, but his voice had abandoned him.

"You're not real," Elias gasped, stepping backward, his breath coming in shallow, rapid bursts.

The thing smiled, its decayed lips peeling back to reveal jagged, rotten teeth. "Neither are you."

The walls closed in, the air pressing against his chest like a suffocating weight. Panic clawed at his ribs. He turned and ran, his boots slamming against the fleshy floor, the walls pressing inward as he sprinted blindly through the ever-shifting corridors. He called out, his voice hoarse. "Maria! Rachel! Janey! Olivia! Where are you?!" But the house absorbed his words, swallowing them into the shadows.

Maria ran through the twisting halls, her vision blurred with terror, the distant sound of the children's humming growing louder. Her lungs burned, her muscles screamed for relief, but she couldn't stop, couldn't let them catch her.

The walls pulsed, closing in around her. The faces of the lost children appeared in the shadows, watching, waiting, grinning. Her breath hitched, a sob breaking free. She was drowning in the overwhelming sensation of being hunted, knowing she was nothing but prey.

A massive, ornate door loomed in front of her. Unlike the shifting, decayed house around her, this door was pristine, gleaming with dark mahogany and brass, untouched by the rot consuming everything else.

Maria hesitated, her fingers trembling as she reached for the handle. Was this another trick?

A child's voice whispered from behind her, too close. "Play the game, Maria. Don't run. Running makes it worse."

The door flung open on its own.

A force yanked Maria forward, pulling her inside.

She landed hard on the floor of what appeared to be a nursery.

The room was sickeningly familiar—her own childhood bedroom.

The air was thick with the scent of dust and something sour. Her bed sat in the corner, small, pink, covered in her favorite childhood blankets. The old rocking chair next to it creaked, moving on its own.

And in that chair sat her mother.

Or something wearing her mother's skin.

"Come sit with me, baby girl," the thing whispered, her voice warping, splitting into two. "You've been running for so long. Aren't you tired?"

Maria pressed her hands against her ears. "You're not her!"

The rocking chair lurched forward, screeching across the wooden floor as the thing lunged for her. Maria screamed, scrambling backward, her body shaking violently, her mind racing. Was she going to die here? Was this how it ended?

Rachel sat frozen at the dining table, her hands clenching the arms of the chair as the darkness beneath the table slithered closer. The missing players around her didn't move, didn't blink, their glassy eyes fixed on her like she was the final course of a meal.

A fork clattered to the ground.

The shadows reacted.

They lunged, wrapping around her ankles, pulling her down.

She screamed, thrashing as the cold, damp tendrils dragged her under the table, into the abyss waiting below. The air was thick, suffocating, the weight of countless lost souls pressing against her like a thousand invisible hands. Screaming. Laughing. Begging.

Rachel clawed at the wooden surface above her, her nails splitting as she tried to find something, anything to grab onto. Her chest burned, her lungs emptying in a panicked gasp. She was sinking, being consumed by the very thing that had taken them all before her.

Then, a hand reached down.

A real hand.

Elias.

"Take it!" he roared, straining as he leaned over the edge, his eyes wild, desperate.

Rachel didn't hesitate. She lunged, her fingers slamming into his palm.

The shadows shrieked.

Elias pulled with all his strength, yanking her up as the darkness writhed and lashed, furious at being denied its prey. Rachel collapsed against him, gasping, her entire body shaking violently.

"We have to find the others," Elias said, his grip tightening around her wrist. "Now."

Janey's world spun.

The maze shifted with every step she took, the hedges growing taller, darker, suffocating her.

The Housekeeper stood a few feet ahead, smiling.

"You can't win, Janey," he said, his voice smooth, amused. "The game has already chosen its victors."

Janey clenched her jaw, her nails biting into her palm as she held her next card tightly. "Then why are you still playing?"

The Housekeeper's smile widened. "Because it's fun."

The wind howled through the maze, but it wasn't wind.

It was screaming.

Janey's stomach lurched as something grabbed her ankle from beneath the hedge. She gasped, staggering back as hands shot from the ground, clawing at her skin, pulling, digging.

The Housekeeper tilted his head, watching. "Play your hand, Janey. Or let them take you."

Janey's fingers trembled as she lifted the card. She had no choice.

The ground beneath her split open.

She was falling, the darkness swallowing her whole.

The house was winning.

The walls trembled, the corridors stretched, the voices of the lost screaming in a relentless chorus. The Housekeeper watched from the shadows, smiling.

Elias and Rachel stumbled forward, desperate, terrified. Somewhere in the distance, Maria screamed. Janey's cry echoed from the abyss.

The next move was theirs.

And the game was far from over.

Twenty-Two

The house was no longer just playing with them—it was consuming them.

The walls pulsed with thick, black veins, writhing like a nest of snakes beneath the rotting wallpaper. A rancid, humid breath exhaled from the very foundation, carrying the scent of decay and something deeper—something ancient, festering beneath the surface of reality. The air pressed down, thick filling their lungs with horrors.

Elias and Rachel stumbled through the corridor, their bodies battered, their minds fraying at the edges. Elias's hands trembled violently, his fingers slick with sweat and something darker—blood, though he couldn't tell if it was his own.

"Keep moving," Elias rasped, his throat raw, his voice a ghost of its former strength. Every fiber of his being screamed for him to stop, to collapse, to surrender, but he couldn't.

Rachel clung to him, her fingers digging into his forearm as she tried to focus through the ringing in her skull. The shadows around them slithered and coiled like living things, licking at their heels, whispering their names in voices that didn't belong to anyone they knew.

"We have to get to Maria and Janey," she gasped, her breath coming in sharp, uneven bursts. "We have to end this."

A violent boom rattled the walls, and then a deep, guttural sound—laughter.

Not human.

Not entirely real.

The Housekeeper was near.

Maria's world was collapsing around her. The nursery wasn't a nursery anymore.

The walls had melted into writhing slabs of flesh, pulsing and breathing, stitched together with rusty nails and black sinew. The ceiling had peeled away, revealing an endless void of writhing shapes twisting, shifting, reaching. The crib in the corner rocked violently, slamming against the wall, though there was nothing inside—nothing visible.

The thing that wore her mother's face loomed closer, its limbs stretching, bending in ways that no human body ever should. Its jaw cracked open, widening far beyond its natural limit, revealing rows of black, jagged teeth, gnashing, grinding.

"Come home, Maria," it crooned in a voice that cracked and splintered like old wood. "You never should have left."

Maria's entire body trembled. Every part of her wanted to collapse, to close her eyes and let this thing take her—because fighting felt impossible.

But she wasn't that girl anymore.

With a scream ripped from the deepest pit of her being, Maria lunged forward, grabbing the rocking chair and swinging it as hard as she could. The wood splintered against the thing's face, but it only laughed—a shrieking, unnatural sound that burrowed into her bones.

Then, the hands came.

Hundreds of them, erupting from the walls, from the crib, from the floor, reaching for her. Grabbing. Clawing.

Maria shrieked as fingers buried themselves into her arms, yanking her downward. Into the floor.

She fought, kicked, clawed, but the hands were stronger. The voices sang to her, sweet and horrible.

"Stay. Stay. Stay. Stay."

Her body convulsed as the fingers dragged her deeper. The pressure against her chest was unbearable, the cold touch of a hundred figures pulling her into their grasp. Her breath hitched in short, panicked gasps, her limbs growing heavier, sinking. The last of the nursery faded into a haze of darkness, the distorted echoes of her childhood merging with the nightmarish now.

Her screams turned silent.

Janey's body slammed against something hard, her breath ripping from her lungs as she crashed into the endless black abyss.

She wasn't falling anymore.

But she wasn't standing either.

The air around her was thick, almost gelatinous, pressing in on her, holding her still. Her limbs twitched, but she couldn't move. Couldn't breathe. Couldn't scream.

Then, the whispering started.

Hundreds of voices, speaking all at once.

Not to her—about her.

"She's weak."

"She doesn't belong."

"She'll never make it out."

Something moved in the darkness.

No. Not something. Many things.

She couldn't see them, but she could hear them, feel them. Long, spindly limbs brushing against her skin, twisting around her wrists, pressing cold fingers against her face.

A shape emerged in the dark. No eyes. No mouth. Just a void.

It tilted its head.

Then, it lunged.

Pain ripped through her as claws tore into her flesh, raking down her arms, her legs. It wasn't just pain—it was worse. It was erasing her, pulling pieces of her away. She could feel herself unraveling, dissolving into the blackness around her.

Her mind fought against it, but her body was betraying her, her strength slipping like sand through her fingers. The more she struggled, the more the darkness gripped her, whispering that she was nothing, that she had always been nothing.

She didn't want to die here.

Elias and Rachel turned a corner and saw her.

Maria, half-sunken into the floor, her eyes wild with terror, her hands clawing at the air.

"Help me!" she screamed, her voice raw, ragged.

Elias didn't think. He dove.

Rachel grabbed Maria's arm just as the hands tightened their grip, trying to pull her under. The shadows screamed in fury as Elias yanked her up, ripping her free just as the floor collapsed inward, a gaping hole of nothingness swallowing the place where she had just been.

Maria shook violently, tears streaking down her face, her body covered in dark, bruising handprints. She could barely speak, her voice hoarse. "I—I was—I thought—"

Rachel hugged her. "We're still here. You're still here."

The moment shattered.
A figure loomed in the doorway.
The Housekeeper.
Tall. Smiling. Waiting.
"Shall we begin the final round?" he purred.
The house groaned, its foundation trembling.
Janey gasped awake, suspended in nothing, her body weightless.
A single card floated before her.
Her move.
Her choice.
Her fate.
With trembling fingers, she reached for it.
And the game prepared for its final move.

Twenty-Three

The house was shifting again, walls stretching and contorting, corridors closing in on themselves only to unfold in new, twisted directions. The game was reaching its climax, and it was no longer content with playing by the rules. It wanted to finish them.

Elias held tightly to Maria and Rachel, pulling them away from the gaping void where the floor had collapsed. Maria's breath came in short, panicked gasps, her body trembling against him. Rachel's grip was iron-clad around his wrist, her fingers digging in, grounding herself in the only reality that still felt stable. The weight of their survival pressed heavily on all of them, a crushing force that made every breath feel like it could be their last.

"We need to find Janey," Elias said, his voice strained but firm. His muscles ached from exertion, but the surge of adrenaline forced him forward. "The Housekeeper's playing his final hand. We don't have much time."

Maria wiped at the bruises forming on her arms, her entire body aching from the grip of the hands. Every inch of her felt like it had been torn apart and stitched back together incorrectly, her nerves still buzzing from the sensation of being pulled into the floor. "How do we even know where to go? This place—" she choked on her words, glancing at the walls that pulsed like living organs, "—it keeps changing. We could be walking straight into another trap."

Rachel swallowed hard, her eyes darting from the shifting walls to the endless blackness behind them. The house wasn't just a structure anymore; it was a living entity, a beast that was closing in, waiting for them to make a mistake. "No, it wants us to think that. But the game has rules, even if they're buried in all this madness. Janey is still playing, which means she has to be somewhere."

A low groan rumbled through the house, and the very floor beneath them quivered. The Housekeeper's presence was thick in the air, cloying and suffocating. The final round had begun.

Janey felt herself suspended in nothingness, the void stretching infinitely in all directions. Cold fingers still lingered on her skin, brushing over her shoulders, her arms, her face—always present but never quite solid. Her body felt weightless, yet the crushing sense of dread anchored her in place, an unbearable tension building inside her chest.

The voices were relentless, whispering from all angles, each one slicing into her mind like a thousand tiny needles.

"You've lost."

"You don't belong here."

"No one is coming for you."

The darkness slithered over her like living tar, suffocating, pressing against her ribs, slipping between her fingers. It was a drowning sensation, slow and inevitable. She was being erased, piece by piece, the house stripping away her very existence.

But then—
A sound cut through the abyss.
Her name.
Distant but clear.

Her heart leaped in her chest. Elias. Rachel. Maria. They were still fighting. They were looking for her.

She clenched her teeth, forcing her hands into fists. No. She wasn't going to let this thing take her. Not when the others were still trying. Not when she still had a choice.

She reached forward into the darkness, her fingers brushing against something solid. A single playing card floated before her, its edges glowing faintly in the void. The final move.

Her hand trembled as she reached for it. The darkness screamed in protest, shrieking and clawing at her, trying to pull her back into its embrace. The pressure intensified, threatening to break her bones, crush her lungs. But Janey's grip closed around the card, and for the first time since she had been dragged into the abyss, she felt something shift.

The game was still being played.
And she was still in it.

The walls convulsed, the air thick with static as Elias, Maria, and Rachel pushed forward. The hallways twisted, bending around them, trying to divert their path. Doors appeared only to vanish the second they got close, the house teasing them, baiting them, daring them to lose hope.

Elias clenched his jaw, his voice raw. "Janey! Can you hear me?!"

Somewhere far ahead, a sound rippled through the void. A single note, like the flick of a card against a table. And then —

A scream.

Maria's breath hitched. "That's her."

Rachel's fingers curled into fists. "Then we run."

They sprinted forward, ignoring the way the ground beneath them felt wrong—like running on something not quite solid, something that shifted beneath their weight. The walls groaned, reaching for them, clawing at their skin as they forced their way through the ever-changing maze. The entire house seemed to be watching, waiting for them to falter.

Then, suddenly, the corridor ended.

A single door stood before them, tall and heavy, etched with intricate carvings of playing cards and symbols they didn't understand. The final room.

A whisper slid through the air, curling around them like smoke.

"One last turn."

Elias pushed open the door, and the three of them stepped inside.

And there, at the center of the room, was Janey.

She was kneeling, gripping something in her hands, her face twisted with determination and terror. Her knuckles were white, her entire body trembling with the weight of the choice before her. She lifted her head at the sound of the door creaking open, and relief washed over her eyes, her breath hitching.

"You made it," she gasped, her voice breaking.

Elias stepped forward, but before he could reach her, a figure materialized between them.

The Housekeeper.

He stood tall, impossibly still, his tailored suit unruffled, his expression the same unreadable calm as always. But his eyes gleamed with something new—anticipation.

He smiled, hands folded neatly in front of him. "All players accounted for," he said smoothly. "Shall we see who wins?"

The walls trembled, the house exhaling a deep, guttural breath. The final play was here.

The game was reaching its conclusion, and whatever happened next would determine who made it out—and who never would.

Twenty-Four

The house groaned around them, its walls trembling with anticipation, feeding off their fear, their desperation. The final round had begun, and the Housekeeper stood between them and their only chance at survival. The very air vibrated with energy, the weight of countless souls pressing against the fragile boundaries of this game. It felt as though time itself had been stretched thin, seconds dragging like hours, the atmosphere thick with an ancient presence that had no intention of letting them go.

Janey's fingers tightened around the card in her hands, her knuckles turning white as she forced herself to breathe through the suffocating dread clawing at her chest. The card pulsed with energy, radiating heat through her fingers, as if the very fabric of the game was aware that this was it—the moment that would decide everything. Her heartbeat pounded in her ears, a steady, frantic rhythm that was at war with the unnatural silence pressing in around them.

Elias, Maria, and Rachel stood just feet away, but they felt impossibly far, as if the Housekeeper himself had stretched the space between them, bending the rules to keep them from reaching her. The ground beneath them was no longer solid, shifting and undulating as though they were standing on the stomach of some great beast waiting to devour them whole.

"You've played well," the Housekeeper mused, his voice calm, smooth, his expression untouched by the chaos unraveling around them. His eyes gleamed with something unnatural, something cold and ancient. "Better than most. But every game must have a winner. And a price."

Elias took a slow step forward, his body tense, his muscles coiled like a predator ready to strike. "The game's over. We're done playing."

The Housekeeper let out a soft chuckle. "Oh, Elias. You don't get to decide when it's over."

With a flick of his wrist, the walls convulsed, splitting apart as shadowy figures poured into the room. They were grotesque, twisted versions of the players who had lost before them, their bodies warped and stretched, their faces frozen in eternal screams. Their eyes glowed with the same eerie light as the cards, their movements jerky and unnatural as they stalked toward them. Some of them still wore remnants of the lives they had before—the tattered dress of a girl who had once been someone's daughter, the frayed jacket of a man who had hoped to win but had failed. The echoes of their suffering lingered in the air, turning the very atmosphere into something heavy, suffocating.

Rachel's breath caught in her throat, her fingers trembling as she pulled Maria closer. "Tell me we can fight them."

Maria swallowed hard, her voice barely a whisper. "I don't know."

The Housekeeper raised his hand, and the creatures lunged.

Elias barely had time to react before one of them was on him, its clawed fingers digging into his shoulder as he twisted away, shoving it back with everything he had. The moment it hit the ground, it convulsed, its limbs contorting as if something inside it was breaking apart. But it didn't stop. It never stopped. It rose again, its soulless gaze fixed on Elias as though it had already claimed him.

Rachel swung at one with a broken chair leg she had grabbed from the ground, the impact sending it reeling, but it barely seemed to register the blow. The thing turned its head with a sickening crack and lunged again, forcing her backward. She stumbled, barely keeping her footing, as another figure clawed at her arm, its bony fingers like ice against her skin.

Maria screamed as another lunged at her, its gaping mouth stretching wider than it should have been possible. She kicked at it, scrambling backward, feeling the cold press of shadows against her spine. The sound of its distorted breathing filled her ears, and for a moment, she thought she felt the shape of fingers wrap around her throat.

"Janey!" Elias shouted, his voice raw, desperate. "Play the damn card!"

Janey's breath came in short gasps, her fingers tightening around the card. The Housekeeper's grin widened, his hands folding neatly in front of him as if he were merely an amused spectator watching his favorite show reach its climax.

"Are you sure?" he taunted. "Do you even know what move you're making? What you're risking?"

Janey's pulse roared in her ears, drowning out the screams, the groans, the relentless shifting of the house as it fed off their suffering. She had no idea what this card would do, what choice she was actually making. But she did know one thing—if she didn't do something now, none of them were getting out alive.

She lifted the card and slammed it onto the ground.

A shockwave erupted from where it landed, sending a deep, shuddering pulse through the house. The creatures shrieked, their bodies convulsing, some dissolving into the very shadows that had birthed them. The walls groaned, fracturing as the house seemed to recoil from the force Janey had just unleashed.

The Housekeeper's smile faltered.

Elias took the chance and lunged.

His fist collided with the Housekeeper's jaw, sending him staggering backward. It wasn't much, but it was enough. Enough to break the illusion of untouchability that had surrounded him, enough to prove that he could be hurt.

"You think this changes anything?" the Housekeeper sneered, straightening, his voice still eerily composed despite the crack forming along the edge of his carefully crafted demeanor.

The house trembled again, but this time, it wasn't the Housekeeper's doing.

It was Janey's move.

The walls began to collapse inward, the corridors folding, the ceiling splintering as the foundation cracked apart. The house was falling. The game was breaking.

But they still weren't free.

The Housekeeper turned toward them, and for the first time, something flickered in his gaze. Something close to irritation. "You don't know what you've done."

Rachel grabbed Maria's hand, pulling her toward the doorway that was beginning to crack open beyond the ruined walls. "Whatever it is, I think we're about to find out."

The air around them howled as the shadows fought to hold themselves together, trying to reform, to regain control. But something deeper was at work now, something unraveling the very fabric of the game itself.

Elias locked eyes with the Housekeeper, his chest heaving. "You lose."

The Housekeeper's lips curled. "Do I?"

And then, in the chaos, came the whisper. The one sound that stopped Elias cold.

A voice he knew.

A voice they all knew.

"You really thought it would be that easy?"

Twenty-Five

The house was dying. The very walls trembled, fractures splintering through the air like bones snapping in the dark. The ceiling groaned, beams bending under force, dust and rot raining from above as the entity that had lived here for centuries fought against its own unraveling. The game was breaking apart, unraveling at the seams, but they weren't safe yet.

Not with the figure standing before them.

Janey's breath hitched in her throat, her chest heaving, her fingers twitching as her mind fought to comprehend the horror before her. The one pulling the strings all along. The one who had kept them playing, leading them through the nightmare, forcing them deeper into the house's grip.

It was impossible. It had to be impossible.

Rachel's lips parted, but no sound came out. She took a slow step back, her pulse pounding so hard it roared in her ears. "You can't be—"

The figure before them smiled, their expression eerily serene.

"Surprised?" the voice was familiar, twisted with something unnatural, something old. "Come now. You should have known."

Maria's hands clenched into fists. "No, this isn't real. You're a trick, another illusion of the house. You can't be—"

"I am," the betrayer interrupted smoothly. "And I always have been."

The moonlight cut through the shifting debris of the house, illuminating the figure's face. The realization hit like a sledgehammer, a force so strong Maria nearly staggered.

It was Miriam.

The head of the coven. The one who had guided them, who had promised help. The one who had sworn to stop the game.

But she had never meant to stop it. She had only ever meant to control it.

Elias's stomach twisted with fury. "You—" his voice caught in his throat, his hands trembling with restrained rage. "You knew what this was. And you still—"

Miriam's eyes gleamed, unnatural and endless. "Of course I knew. I was there when it was born."

The ground beneath them cracked, pulsing with something ancient. The very essence of the house groaned, as if reacting to the truth finally surfacing.

"I made this game," Miriam admitted, tilting her head as if she was simply reminiscing. "A long time ago, before the coven, before your little town ever existed. It started as an experiment, a way to test the limits of power. But it became something more. Something... alive."

Janey's hands shook violently at her sides. "You sacrificed people. You made them play. You let them die."

Miriam's face remained calm. "I didn't make them do anything. They chose to play. Just like you did. Just like everyone before you."

Rachel's voice wavered, barely above a whisper. "Then why us? Why now?"

Miriam's gaze darkened. "Because you were strong enough. And if you were strong enough to survive, you were strong enough to replace me."

Maria let out a breath, ragged and furious. "You wanted a successor."

"Not wanted," Miriam corrected. "Needed. I am bound to the game, just as the Housekeeper was. Someone must always run the game, just as someone must always play."

The shadows slithered closer, whispering, hungry.

Miriam raised her hand, and a deck of cards materialized in her palm, shifting as if each card contained something writhing beneath its surface. "And now, it's time for you to choose."

Elias stepped forward, his fists clenched. "We're not playing your game. We're ending it."

Miriam's lips curled into a smile. "Oh, Elias," she sighed. "You should know by now—you don't end the game. The game ends you."

The ground exploded beneath them.

Darkness surged outward, engulfing them all. The walls shattered, the sky itself seemed to crack, and from the abyss of the house, something rose.

The entity.

It had no form, no face, only presence. It wrapped itself around Miriam, seeping into her veins, coursing through her skin. She let out a shuddering breath, eyes rolling back, as the game fed on her.

And then—she changed.

Her body contorted, elongated, shadows weaving into her flesh like a puppet being re-stitched by invisible strings. Her bones cracked, her eyes bled black, her mouth twisted into something that was no longer human.

Miriam was no longer just Miriam.

She was the game itself.

And she was hungry.

Rachel screamed as a tendril of darkness lashed toward her, knocking her back. Elias barely had time to pull Maria out of the way before another tendril crashed into the ground where she had stood.

"RUN!" Elias roared.

But there was nowhere to run. The house was closing in.

Janey's hands trembled as she reached into her pocket—her last card, the one she had stolen in secret, the one she had hoped she'd never need to use.

"This ends now," she whispered, voice shaking.

Miriam—the thing Miriam had become—laughed. "You can't stop it. You never could."

Janey's fingers dug into the card. "Then we die trying."

She threw it down.

A violent wind roared through the space. The entity screamed, recoiling, splintering apart as if something inside it had just cracked beyond repair. The very structure of the house folded inward, warping as the game itself fought against the command.

Miriam shrieked, her body fracturing, the darkness unraveling from her form like a cocoon being violently ripped away.

"No!" she howled, her voice twisting into something more than human, more than mortal. "I am the game! You can't—!"

But she was already fading.

The walls collapsed. The sky tore apart.

And the house died.

Then—

Silence.

Rachel coughed, dust and debris filling her lungs as she forced herself up, her limbs trembling. Elias lay beside her, his breathing heavy but alive.

Maria wiped blood from her lips, pushing herself onto her elbows, gasping for air.

Janey stood in the wreckage, her fingers still curled as if she could feel the weight of the card dissolving in her hand. Her breath came in short, sharp bursts as she looked around at what remained.

The house was gone.

Miriam was gone.

And the game… was over.

The sky above them was clear. The sun was rising, painting the world in soft hues of pink and gold. A new day.

They had won.

And yet—

Janey's gaze lowered to the ground, to the single, untouched card resting at her feet. The edges flickered, shifting, waiting.

A new game.

A new invitation.

Her breath hitched.

She bent down—hesitated—then, with shaking fingers, she picked it up.
A whisper caressed her ear.
"Do you want to play?"
Janey stared at the card.
And then—
She tore it in half.
The wind howled.
The card vanished.
The game… was finally over.

AFTERMATH

The town would never be the same. Elias stood at the edge of what had once been the cursed mansion, the ruins still smoldering beneath the weight of its own demise. The air was thick with the scent of burned wood and damp earth, the remnants of something far older than time itself finally exorcised from the land. But even now, in the silence of the wreckage, a feeling lingered—something was watching, waiting.

Janey stood beside him, her arms wrapped tightly around herself, as if bracing against the invisible weight of what they had survived. Her knuckles were raw, her face lined with exhaustion. She had barely spoken since they had left the house, since she had torn the card in half, since she had chosen to defy the game in its final move.

"Do you think it's really over?" Rachel asked, her voice barely above a whisper. Her hands trembled as she wiped the soot from her arms, her body still aching from the ordeal.

Elias didn't answer right away. He wanted to believe it was over. He wanted to think that nothing like this could happen again. But the truth lay heavy in his chest, dark and unrelenting.

"We don't take chances," he said finally, his jaw tightening. "Not with something like this."

Janey exhaled, turning to look at him, her expression unreadable. "Then we make sure it never happens again."

And so, a vow was made that night, beneath the cold moon of a town that would never truly know the horrors that had nearly swallowed it whole. Elias and Janey took it upon themselves to watch over the town, to ensure that no child, no wandering soul, would ever stumble too close to the game again. The coven, now free of Miriam's twisted influence, swore to bind what little remnants of its magic still lingered, to make sure the house could never reform, that the whispers would never call again.

Weeks passed. The town moved on. The house became nothing more than an old legend, a ghost story parents told to keep their children from straying too far from home. But those who had survived knew better.

The game had lived for centuries. And things like that don't just die.

It was late one autumn evening when three children stood at the edge of the ruins. The moon hung low, bathing the skeletal remains of the house in pale light. The wind whispered through the trees, curling around them like talons, beckoning.

"They say it was a haunted house," one of the boys murmured, his breath fogging in the cold air. "That people used to disappear here."

The girl beside him shivered, hugging her jacket closer. "Maybe we shouldn't be here."

The third child, the tallest of the three, smirked. "What's the worst that could happen? It's just a house. It's not like it's still... alive."

And then—

A sound. A groan from beneath the earth. A deep, shuddering exhale, as if the house had simply been waiting.

The heavy oak doors, untouched and unscathed despite the ruins surrounding them, creaked open.

An invitation.

The children froze, their wide eyes reflecting the shifting darkness beyond the threshold. The air around them thickened, the scent of dust and something older than time itself curling at their feet. The game had always been patient. It had always been waiting.

And now, it was ready to play again.

"Do you want to play?"

The whisper curled around them like smoke.

The doors stood open.

And the children took their first step inside.

Truth or Dare

"Where the Magic Happens"

Ladies and gentlemen, step right up to "Where the Magic Happens" - a literary circus that'll make your bookshelf do backflips! Meet Patti, the ringmaster of this wordy wonderland! She's not just an Executive Producer; she's a word-wrangling wizard, conjuring up an animated TV series based on "ELLIOT FINDS A HOME." It's the tail-wagging tale of a thumbs-up pup and his silent sidekick, proving that you don't need words when you've got opposable digits and a heart of gold! Hold onto your bestseller lists, folks! This Polygon Entertainment superstar has hit the USA TODAY jackpot and Amazon's #1 spot more times than a cat has lives.

With 8 dozen books under her belt, she's got more genres than a chameleon has colors. From Urban Fantasy to Horror, she's been spinning yarns longer than your grandma's knitting needles! But wait, there's more!

Patti's life is like a celebrity bingo card: She rocked "Romper Room" at 4, probably making the other kids look like amateur rompers. She rubbed elbows with Captain Kangaroo and Mr. Green Jeans. (No word on whether the jeans were actually green.) She shared a train ride and a sandwich with Sidney Poitier. Talk about a meal ticket to stardom! She high-fived President Nixon at the circus. Who knew the circus could get any more political? She went to school with David Copperfield. We assume she didn't disappear during attendance. She roller-skated with pre-famous John Travolta. Grease lightning, indeed!

She sipped cocoa with Abe Vigoda. Fish never tasted so sweet! When she's not busy being a literary legend, Patti's juggling roles faster than a circus performer. Teacher, grandma, furparent - she does it all with a smile that could light up a haunted house.

Speaking of haunted houses, meet the "Queen of Halloween" herself! This Wiccan High Priestess is stirring up stories spookier than a skeleton's dance moves. Her books are flying off the shelves faster than witches on broomsticks, so follow her on social media or risk missing out on the hocus-pocus!

So, come one, come all, to Patti's phantasmagorical world of words! It's more exciting than a roller coaster, more magical than a rabbit in a hat, and more diverse than a box of assorted chocolates. Don't be shy - step into the spotlight and join the literary party where the pages turn themselves and the stories never end!

www.ingramcontent.com/pod-product-compliance
Lightning Source LLC
LaVergne TN
LVHW092048060526
838201LV00047B/1299